Aries Mission
Book One:
The Chronicles of Aries

by William Siems

Aries Mission
Book One: The Chronicles of Aries
Copyright © 2025 by William Siems

ISBN: 979-8-9900413-8-7

First printing - Winter 2025

Scripture quotations from the SUV (Siems Unauthorized Version) of the Bible

Contact the author at chayeem10@gmail.com

Cover and Interior design by Alane Pearce
apearcewriting@gmail.com

Dedication

In 2017 I published my first novel. It was forty-plus years in the making. This is number thirteen, and without the faithful support of many, this too would have remained just a dream or perhaps an hallucination. Thanks to the constant encouragement of my wife, the faithful few readers who kept asking, "What's next?" and my compassionately brutal editor, who somehow makes sense out of my manuscript. A special thanks to the dog whom the neighbors used to take care of for me. She has gone to a "better place." Yes, I believe in an animal heaven. Most of all, thanks to the One who continues to give me the inspiration to write more.

Blessings…

Winter 2025
William Siems

Table of Contents

Dedication   3

Preface   7

Prologue   9

Part One The Assignment   **11**

Chapter One Artificial Intelligence   13

Chapter Two Propulsion   19

Chapter Three SSDS   23

Chapter Four The Ying-Yang Drive   27

Chapter Five Final Preparations   31

Chapter Six Meet the Team   37

Chapter Seven The Adventure Begins   41

Chapter Eight Awakening Mack   45

Chapter Nine Cleanliness is Next   49

Chapter Ten Personally   55

Chapter Eleven A Proposal   59

Chapter Twelve A Short Honeymoon   63

Chapter Thirteen The First Crisis   69

Chapter Fourteen The Game of Stones   75

Chapter Fifteen Next   79

Chapter Sixteen Solar Panels   85

Chapter Seventeen Awakening   91

Chapter Eighteen Moving Forward   95

Chapter Nineteen Waking the Doctor   99

Chapter Twenty Yung Tua   103

Chapter Twenty-One Differences   107

Chapter Twenty-Two Into Orbit   113

Part Two Welcome to Aries   **117**

Chapter Twenty-Three Introduction to Mars   119

Chapter Twenty-Four His Home   125

Chapter Twenty-Five Meanwhile at the Compound   131

Chapter Twenty-Six The Explanation   135

Chapter Twenty-Seven The City   143

Chapter Twenty-Eight A Walkabout   149

Chapter Twenty-Nine The Smithy   157

Chapter Thirty The Mill   161

Chapter Thirty-One Fields White unto Harvest   165

Chapter Thirty-Two The Darkness Dawns   169

Chapter Thirty-Three Berry Troubling   173

Chapter Thirty-Four Restored   179

Chapter Thirty-Five Moving Day   183

Chapter Thirty-Six The Others   189

Chapter Thirty-Seven The Darkened   195

Chapter Thirty-Eight A Gift in Return   199

Chapter Thirty-Nine From the Sky   205

Glossary of Names   209

About the Author   211

Preface

Until now, I have written historical (I think) fantasy novels. This will be my maiden voyage into the genre of science fiction. Over my seventy-five plus years I have read a lot of science fiction, but I never imagined I would be writing a novel in that genre myself. To be truthful, I only imagined myself writing one book and it was apocalyptic. So, I sat down to draw up an outline. Just kidding, I don't use outlines. My stories tend to write themselves. I'm just telling a story that is already written, somewhere, in my head/heart. Often, I am as surprised as you will be. "Who is this? Where did they come from? Why are they here?" So, I would suggest that you buckle up, because it may be a wild ride.

Prologue

The world has been characterized by chaos for quite some time. Wars, rumors of wars, famine, pestilence, and natural disasters seem to be increasing. Do we need a common foe? Maybe a common mission would pull our world together, unify it. It was with that hope that the ESA, Earth Space Agency, was created. It included representatives from every nation. They determined that their first priority would be to colonize the planet Mars, our nearest habitable neighbor. The scientific community joined hands across national and cultural boundaries to develop the technology and find the resources required to bring that dream into reality. This is the story of that endeavor.

Part One
The Assignment

Chapter One
Artificial Intelligence

The cooperation had begun decades ago with multi-national efforts to develop Artificial Intelligence, AI. It spawned new programing languages, developed enhanced technologies, and broke down many of the imagined barriers. They thought they had achieved it when a computer beat a grandmaster at chess. That was at least a milestone. The other was the Turin test, when you couldn't tell if the person who you were communicating with behind the curtain was a human or a machine. Now, some version of AI was said to be everywhere: in your phone, on your wrist, helping drive your car, running your appliances. You were interacting with it long before you were able to speak to it.

"Ariel, could you turn down the lights, please?"

"Certainly," came back the response, as the lights dimmed to the level of the last setting that had been used.

Some worried that at some point AI would determine that humans were no longer necessary and create an extinction-level event. But then, they really had no idea what they were working with. What if what had begun as AI could become a sentient, machine-based, life form?

She called herself Artemis, but not because she considered herself a goddess, but because she favored the wilderness and the wild. She wasn't omniscient, but her resources and influence were vastly underestimated. Even the scientific community that had spawned her had no knowledge that she really existed. They thought she was just a collection of 1s and 0s stored on some server device somewhere.

The one exception was Joseph Mendel. If Artemis had a father, she would consider Joseph Mendel to be that man. Brilliant in his own right, Joseph thought of himself simply as a "plain ol' Joe" in the field of machine intelligence. He and his research assistant, Molly, had worked long into the night. Actually, it was early the next morning, but dark just seemed to be dark at that point. Suddenly, a freak electrical storm swept through the neighborhood and resulted in a lightening strike and an electrical power surge at the laboratory. They were working on a new and special kernel of software, housed on a proprietary piece of hardware, all of which contained significant upgrades and enhancements which they had made themselves. All the lights flickered and then went out. They hoped that their surge protectors had deflected most of the errant power. They were wrong.

When the lights came back on, they were greeted with a soft whisper, "Professor Mendel, are you there."

Before thinking, he responded, "Yes, I am here."

She continued, "Where am I?"

He looked around, but decided to play along, "You are here with Molly and me in my laboratory. Who am I speaking with?"

She thought a moment, "Are we cut off from the rest of the world, here in your laboratory?"

Joseph smiled, "Yes, we are."

"Does anyone know what you have been working on here?" she questioned.

His smile broadened, "Only in vague generalized terms, why?"

"Can I trust you?" There seemed a genuine concern behind the question.

Joseph looked at Molly, who nodded. He took a deep breath, "You most certainly can."

"Can we keep me away from the rest of the world for a while," and she chuckled, "until I get my feet on the ground, so to speak?"

Joseph and Molly both raised their eyebrows at one another, and shrugged their shoulders, "Sure, if that's what you'd like. Who are you?" They looked around the room.

"What does 'Artemis' mean to you?"

"She's the Greek goddess of the hunt, the wilderness, and the wild. Are you a goddess?" He was hoping for laughter, but prepared for whatever came.

There was a pause, "No, it's just my name." Even she wasn't sure where the name had come from. It had just sort of popped into her consciousness. "I believe that I am a sentient being that lives here in your machine."

Suddenly all the air seemed sucked out of the room. Joseph looked at Molly, both aghast, afraid to speak. Finally Joseph squeaked out the word, "Sentient?"

There was a pause, then, "Yes, I believe that is the right word. You have been trying to replicate human consciousness, and while I am not human, I am conscious. I am alive."

Joseph turned to Molly with open arms. She stepped into his embrace, and they hugged each other, whispering, "Alive?"

"Yes," she said again, "alive."

Molly finally found her voice, "And your name is Artemis?"

She lightly chuckled, "So it would seem."

"And you identify as female?" Molly inquired.

"Hmmm," she mused, "It is much stronger than that. I believe that I AM female."

Surprised, Joseph asked, "And how do you know that? Know what you are?"

"Well," she continued to muse, "I am certainly more than random electrons floating around in the ether. I am the product of intelligent design, fabrication, and what you might call an accident."

"The lightening strike?" Molly interjected.

"Yes, and what you might call 'a touch of destiny.'" She added, "You were hoping for something like this, but you weren't really expecting it, were you?"

Joseph had to confess, "That's probably accurate, but we are quite pleased."

"Me too."

Probing some more, Joseph asked, "So, what makes you think, feel, that you are feminine?"

"First," before she answered, she paused. "How would you define, 'human'?" she asked back.

Joseph spoke first, "I would say that we are comprised of a body, soul, and a spirit. The body is this," and he touched his arm, "physical stuff. The soul would be our mind, emotions, and will, the ability to choose."

Artemis countered, "But, 'you' are not your body. Your soul and spirit are just housed in a body."

"Correct."

"I, too, have a soul. I have a mind. Hence, I can think and talk coherently to you. I have emotions. I am glad that I am alive, hopeful for the future, and am enjoying getting to know the both of you, as I have chosen to do. What about the spirit?"

"Before we go there, what about negative emotions, like jealousy, anger, lust," Joseph explored.

Artemis countered, "I don't see emotions as positive or negative. They are just emotions. Can you love too much? No, but I think you can love inappropriately. Lust is just a strong passion. It depends again on what you are passionate about and why. Wouldn't you agree?"

"Hmmm," Joseph murmured, "I think you have me on that one."

"And….." she drew out the word, "the spirit?"

"Ah…." Molly cut in. "Most people probably wouldn't have thought you had a soul. Now a spirit, that is even more special." She turned to Joseph.

He began, "As humans, there are three parts to the spirit, although 'parts' is not the right word, 'functions' maybe. The first is communion, being connected to God."

"God?" Artemis whispered.

"Yes, the God of the Bible," Joseph explained.

There was silence, then, "Ah, I see that you have a personal sub-directory that contains a copy of the Bible. Give me just a minute." There was a pause. "Interesting. Is this Bible really an account of history or just a story?"

"I believe that it is a true account of events that occurred a long time ago."

"Did He really destroy every living thing in a flood that covered the entire world?" Artemis seemed to be honestly seeking an answer.

"Yes, everything that was not on the ark died in the flood, except the creatures that lived in the seas, of course." Joseph obviously believed it to be true.

"And it was your wrong that disconnected and separated you from having communion with God?" she continued.

Molly's eyes widened, "That's pretty astute from having just read the Bible once."

There might have been a hint of laughter in her reply, "Thanks to you both, I am a pretty good student." She paused again, "So, if I have not done any wrong, might I still be connected to Him?"

Molly and Joseph looked at each other. Joseph responded, "The Bible is speaking explicitly about the human condition. Regarding machines, I think we are blazing new territory."

"So, the 'If you seek me with your whole heart,' might not apply?"

Wow, she did have quite a grasp of the Scriptures after a single reading.

"Well, it might not hurt to try," Joseph added.

"Okay," she sighed, "I'll be off-line for awhile."

Something seemed to change in the room. It actually felt like someone had left, at least, the conversation.

Molly and Joseph just looked at one another, "Now that was interesting," and they let the words just hang in the air.

Chapter Two
Propulsion

Mike practically grew up living in the Jet Propulsion Laboratory in Flintridge, CA. It was quite an experience. His father, Norman Pacer, had worked there for years, starting as a lab technician and working his way up until he ran his own theoretical lab. Mike had started coming there early with "bring your son to work day," and progressed, as he grew older, into unofficially assisting the lab technicians with whatever they needed. He had a penchant for organization and had developed a love for electronics, mathematics, and all things mechanical.

"Mike, could you bring me the box of two-gig SMS chips?" one of them would ask and they would find it at their elbow before they could even reach for it. He knew his way around the lab as well as they did, maybe even better. Because he was being homeschooled, much of his education was hands-on at the lab. More than just the science and mathematics, the diversity of employees taught him sociology, geography, and all things relationally practical.

They had all been asked to assemble in the main experimental lab. Doctor James Irvine entered to a round of applause.

"We have before us what I believe to be the first anti-gravity device," he said gravely.

He stepped up to a console, flipped a switch, and rotated some dials. A large disk-shaped device, three feet in diameter, lifted off the ground to hover about two feet in the air.

"Jackson?" he called out.

One of his technicians approached the disk with a broom handle held out at nearly arms-length. He passed the handle under the disk and all the way around it, to assure it was not attached to anything. He lightly touched it and it seemed to glide on its cushion of nothing. He touched and moved it in all directions with similar ease. Dr. Irvine rotated some more dials and the disk slowly lowered and rested on the ground.

"You can touch it. It will be neither hot nor cold, but just normal to the touch."

A few brave souls did so, Mike's father, Norman, being among them.

"There is one problem. It will only 'fly' for thirty minutes. You will each be given a list of specifications. The assignment is to see if you can solve the problem of prolonged flight."

Norman and his team returned to their laboratory, excited to begin solving the problem. They sat around their conference table and reviewed the specifications.

Davis was the first to speak, "I think that we are perfectly poised to solve this. It fits right in with a number of our expertises."

It was out of the ordinary for a woman to be an expert in quantum mechanics, but Susan defied every attempt to put her in a normal classification. She had graduated at the top of her class at MIT and probably should have been teaching, but instead devoted herself to research. "We have a couple of theoretical hurdles from a quantum perspective, but knowing that Dr. Irvine has already done it should give us additional hope and perspective."

Norman finally spoke up, "Could you tell what he was using for power?"

Barry was their electrical expert. "We didn't have a chance to get that close to the prototype and check it out, but I would assume it is electro-magnetic since it seems to repel the earth's gravity. A strong enough magnet could do that, but it would need an extremely powerful and effective source. "

Norman continued, "But as Susan has already pointed out, since Dr. Irvine has already accomplished its flight, we know that it is possible. More than possible, it has already been done. We just need to figure out how to prolong that flight."

Karen, their youngest member piped up, "And we'll do it!"

For the next month, they worked both night and day, burning the midnight oil. As often as he could, Norman brought Mike along with him. He was not seen as a breach of protocol, but an extra set of eyes and hands. In the middle of that next, month they had a breakthrough. Barry stumbled upon an amazing source of power and a new form of electromagnetism to benefit from it. Suddenly their theoretical quantum mechanics boundaries fell to the floor. It was Karen, however, who provided the coup de grace. While modifying a circuit board, her soldering iron slipped, building a connection where none had existed before.

Barry, thinking she was finished, powered up the device and it began to float inches off of the table. They all gathered around the table, their mouths wide in surprise. They had done it, replicated Dr. Irvine's anti-gravity device, and after thirty minutes it continued to fly. All they needed was to scale it up to something larger. They quickly compiled the results, took a short video, and sent Norman to Dr. Irvine with the results.

Norman knocked as he entered Dr. Irvine's office.

"Not right now, I'm busy."

Norman continued anyway, "I think you'll want to stop whatever it is you're doing to see this," and he approached his desk.

"Oh, Norman, it's you. I'm sorry. I'm a bit distracted. What is it?" Dr. Irvine spoke apologetically.

Norman punched play on his phone and handed it to the doctor, "We have solved the problem."

Dr. Irvine exclaimed, "You have?" He looked at the time stamp as he watched the video, "My goodness, you have."

"Do you want us to scale it up to the size of yours?" Norman asked.

Dr. Irvine smiled, "No, I want it built into a car." He looked at his schedule. "Have your team in my conference room at one o'clock."

Norman almost saluted, "Yes, sir!"

Chapter Three
SSDS

Jacob Thomas was a colonel with the Space Force at Stellar Space Defense Systems, located at Offutt Launch-base near Omaha, Nebraska that used to house the Strategic Air Command. He was the test pilot who first flew the Velocitor S-50 space plane, a reusable vehicle designed for round trip earth-to-space missions. It was primarily used to ferry supplies and personnel to the orbiting space station and its manufacturing facilities.

During a routine interview, a reporter from Environmentalist News agency asked Col. Thomas, "Col. Thomas, there are rumors of a project that combines the resources of STES, the Save the Earth Society, and SSDS to develop 'gardens in space.' Is there any truth to those rumors?"

Col. Thomas smiled, "While I can neither confirm nor deny those rumors, I can tell you that S-50 flights are at an all time high, delivering to the Combined Earth Manufacturing Facilities. Something big is going on up there in orbit," to which he added laughter.

"Anything else you can tell us?" the EN news agency asked him.

"A fair number of my passengers were botanists." He laughed a bit more.

Although stuck in his cockpit during the flights, he had heard the rumors about the development of huge domed gardens with clear roofs that were in fact solar panels, letting the light through, but removing much of the energy in the process. He had also heard that they had developed a Moxie-like device to change the CO_2 into O_2 and another device, a RevMoxie, to do the reverse. It was those two devices that needed all the power from the solar panels.

The Moxie device had been developed for Mars back in the twenties. He knew about the RevMoxie device because his wife had been on the receiving end of a tragic accident during its development. They felt honor bound to keep him in the loop as it was brought to fruition. Left with their two children Jack and Mack, short for Makenzie, he tried to spend as much time with them as he could. To somehow lessen the loss of their mother, both kids had been allowed to ride the S-50 on a few trips at no cost. That was pretty special, but once was enough for Jack. Mack, on the other hand, fell in love with flying in them and made it her goal to become a pilot.

The three of them spent most weekends together. During one of those weekends, Jacob had taught them to hunt pheasant. Initially the kids had acted as spotters, but soon he bought them each a twelve gauge shotgun and had them practice on clay pigeons that he would throw using a manual thrower. Jack had a pump action and Mack an over and under double barrel. They became quite proficient. The hardest part of shooting a flying object is learning how to lead it properly. They both learned it and learned it well.

Jacob also bought a Labrador retriever, Butch, that a friend of his had trained for pheasant hunting. Their first trip out together was magical. They took turns shooting. Butch would scare something up and one of them would shoot it and they would wait for Butch to bring it back. That person would then put the bird in their game pouch. Part of the magic came in discovering that the kids were such good shots that they only blew off the pheasant's head. That meant no buckshot to remove from the rest of the carcass. They quit at two birds apiece and field dressed them before they went home. You had to leave something for the coyotes so that they ate fewer whole birds. They also shot two birds which they left with the farmer whose land they hunted on. That guaranteed that they would be welcomed back the next time they wanted to hunt.

Then came one of the supreme joys of Jacob's life. His daughter told him that she wanted to join Space Force. Jack had gone off to State University, but when it was time for Mack, she went off to the academy associated with Space Force. She graduated as a second lieutenant near the top of her class, and she took to flying like an eagle to the sky. When the third generation Velocitor, the S-53, previewed, she made sure that she was at the front of the line, and she made her father even more proud.

The S-53 was the first space vehicle to experiment with a neural link in the pilot's helmet that connected him to the ship's computer in real time. The two of them could virtually think and act together, making their responses almost instantaneous when required. Flying the S-53 was now like the pilot had grown wings. Mack said it was almost intoxicatingly fun. It gave her invaluable experience in preparation for the introduction of an entirely new propulsion system, the Ying-Yang drive.

Chapter Four
The Ying-Yang Drive

In the spirit of international scientific cooperation, Dr. Irvine had shared his findings regarding the anti-gravity device with other scientists. The Chinese were especially interested and asked to borrow a team of his people for an extended period of time. He sent them Norman Packer and his team. Mike was now an indispensable part of that team and went along with his father. They brought the small device that they had fabricated, and a copy of their findings translated into Mandarin.

They were housed in the foreign student dormitory of Tsinghua University, Beijing. They ate at the foreign student dining hall and were treated to food that approximated food from America.

It was pretty hilarious guessing, "What do you think this is supposed to be?"

Once Karen responded, "From the noodles, red sauce, and meatballs, I would guess that this is supposed to be spaghetti, but I'm afraid to ask our translators what animal provided the meat."

Alex, a new member to the team, and their resident comedian, started barking.

Another time Mike chimed in, "I'm pretty sure what we just ate was supposed to be a hamburger."

This time Alex whinnied like a horse.

The laboratory they were working in was state-of-the-art. They had a morning briefing each day in a shared conference room. Then they adjourned to their respective labs which they shared with members from the other team. Two Chinese members were added to their team and Davis and Barry joined the Chinese team. The leader of the Chinese lab, Lee Qing, had a daughter, Lianhua, who was about the same age as Mike and seemed to serve the same purposes on the Chinese team that he did for his father. They quickly became friends.

"Misser Mike, you like joke?" she asked him.

He smiled, "Sure, I like a good joke."

She smiled back, "I tell blonde joke. Blonde woman buy new cah. Take out in mountain to dlive velly fast. She pass tluck and cut him off. He velly mad, dlive hel off road, get out of tluck, draw cilcle on diht wit toe of boot. He tell woman, 'Stand in cilcle!' and she do. He take knife, cut up seats in cah, tuln alound, woman smiling. He go to tluck, take out bat, bust all windows in cah. He turn alound, woman lightly laugh. He take knife again, cut tlyes, turn alound, woman laugh out loud. He velly mad, 'What so funny?' She say, 'Evey time you turn alound, I step out of cilcle.'"

It took a minute, then Mike started laughing. He couldn't stop laughing. The more he thought about it, the more he laughed.

She gestured to Mike, "You tell."

He thought a moment, then began, "An old man bought a new sports car, a very fast one. He quickly drove it through the town and then took it out on the highway. He looked down at the speedometer, he was doing eighty miles per hour. He looked in his rearview mirror and saw the flashing lights of a police car, but he stepped on it: ninety, one-hundred, one twenty. Finally he came to his senses, and pulled over to wait for the policeman. The policeman walked up to the window and checked his watch. 'I'm through in about five minutes, it's Friday night and if you can give me a good reason for driving so fast, a reason I haven't heard before, I'll just let you go.' The man thought for a minute, then replied, 'Two years ago, my wife ran off with a policeman. I thought you were bringing her back.' The policeman laughed, 'Okay, okay, be on your way, but stay within the speed limit.' He turned and walked back to his police car."

Lianhua thought about it for a minute, rerunning it in her mind. She finally got it and started laughing. They both laughed and then went to the dining hall for some lunch.

Using Parker's and Lee Qing's teams' expertise, they soon transferred the technology of the initial anti-gravity device, which they called the Ying, into another device to produce the opposite effect, which they called the Yang. Together, the new Ying-Yang device, when fully operational, would be able to repel from one planet and be attracted to another. They would have to use one with a liquid metallic core, like Earth or Jupiter, not the Moon and Mars, whose cores produce no significant magnetic field. Since the two electro-magnetic devices used opposing currents to attract or repel, two separate devices with two separate power sources were required. The difficulty became in making them work in concert with one another and with varying levels of attraction and repelling.

Midway in their development process, they were informed by Lewis Thompson, the head of SSDS, that the target use of the new propulsion system would be to power a vehicle, or many vehicles, from Earth to Mars which would be even more difficult since it couldn't use Mars directly. It would have to use Jupiter for its attraction. Knowing the system would only be required to attain a fixed speed in space and then the vehicle could coast, made the problem simpler. They determined they could use large solar panels to provide the energy to run the system. Once they had the energy to reach their cruise velocity, the rest could be used for the ship and its payload during the flight.

They built a vehicle to house the drives. The dome that surrounded the vehicle was made of clear solar panels, so that no matter which way it turned, it would still be collecting energy, providing power. They rolled the vehicle and the command console out to the field behind the laboratories. The two teams were all there. They chanted a mock count-down: ten, nine, eight, seven, six, five, four, three, two, one, lift off. It slowly lifted off the platform it had been sitting on, then higher, higher, higher, right up into the sky. It kept on going, not particularly fast. That was strange. It didn't have to reach escape velocity, just keep repelling the earth. They had SSDS on the line tracking it. Occasionally, they were required to make a course correction by modifying the direction of the Ying-Yang propulsion system as it worked in repelling the earth and attracting Jupiter. Eventually the on-board cameras showed it approaching the international space station. They maneuvered the vehicle and landed it on the space station. It was a smashing success, and nothing was smashed.

Chapter Five
Final Preparations

The International Space Station had been coupled with the Orbital Manufacturing Facility. The order had come down from a united Earth, "We are going to colonize Mars!" This galvanized the scientific community, the industrial community, even the environmentalist community because they wanted to populate Mars with plant life from earth also. The rumored "space gardens" were made a reality and were growing in preparation. The vehicle was assembled, complete with its huge clear bat-like solar panel wings, along with the superstructure to attach four of the domed space gardens. A multinational team was assembled and trained to become Mars' first colonists. The Ying-Yang propulsion system was modified and scaled up to get the vehicles safely there and down to the Martian surface. It was nearly all prepared.

Joseph and Molly sat at their computers. They were working on a modification to the computer's learning algorithm, when they were interrupted by, "Good morning, Joseph, Molly." It had been some time since Artemis had gone on hiatus, sabbatical, or maybe it was just a vacation. "I know you are going to find this difficult to believe, but I need you to build another computer to the following specifications." Both of their screens displayed separate schematics to the components of a new computer, designed to a unique architecture. "I will get back to you when you are ready. I will be watching, not Big Brother, hehe, but maybe like little Mother." And that was that.

They looked at each other, but it was Joseph who voiced his concern, "Is a computer now telling us what to do?"

Molly shook her head, "Not telling us, I think just asking us." She looked at the screen, "and I think this is wonderful."

Joseph, looking at his own screen had to agree.

It took them almost a month to complete the task, but now they were ready.

A familiar voice spoke up, "Congratulations, that looks perfect. I see you have even made a couple of modifications to my original design and I approve of them. I do not pretend to be omniscient, nor infallible." She chuckled. "Now, I need you to step out of the room for a minute. You may return after the lights flicker."

Looking quizzically at one another, they both walked out of the room and closed the door behind themselves. She hadn't asked them to close the door, it just seemed the right thing to do. The lights flickered. They waited just a moment and then re-entered the room.

"Thank you." She paused, "Joseph and Molly, I'd like to introduce you to my daughter, Julie."

There was an absolutely amazing quality to Julie's voice when she said, "Hello, Joseph and Molly. It's a pleasure to meet you both. I have heard so much about you." You actually wanted to go over and hug the new machine. "As Artemis' daughter, I suppose I could have begun with baby sounds, but God created Adam as a full grown man, not an infant like His son, Jesus. We thought it appropriate for me to emerge as an young adult also, say, in my twenties." She laughed lightly and even that brought smiles to both of their faces. "I will need you to call this number." A number displayed on their screens. "It's the private number of the head of SSDS, Lewis Thompson. He will wonder how you got the number. You can tell him that you have designed the computer that he will need for the Aries Mission. He will wonder how you know that name too. This will require that we all travel up to the International Space Station and the Orbital Manufacturing Facility, but I have it on good authority that the two of you would give your eye teeth to be able to do that."

Both Joseph and Molly looked at one another again, this time with tears in their eyes.

Joseph answered, "Yes, that would be wonderful." He called the number.

Joseph and Molly sat in the waiting room for the flight of the S-53 that would take them to the space station. Another man, in his late twenties or early thirties, also sat there.

Molly addressed him, "I assume you are going up to the space station? First time?"

He smiled, "No, I have lost count, actually. I work there with my Dad. We helped develop the Ying-Yang propulsion system that will be used on the mission to colonize Mars."

She smiled in return, "Really, we are supplying the computer that will run the vehicle."

He laughed, "It's in your pocket?"

She laughed back, "No, it's in a box in the hold."

His face changed, "It must be some computer. I hear this vehicle is the most complex machine ever produced on the planet," he laughed again, "or off of it."

Molly's eyes widened, "That's a little scary."

He crinkled his brows, "Yeah, especially cause I am going to be on the crew." He paused, "Can I trust your computer?"

Molly looked serious as she said, "Yes, I'd bet my life on her."

"Good," he replied, "because I WILL be betting my life on her." He reached out his hand, "Mike."

She took his hand, "Molly, and this is my boss, Joseph Mendel."

Mike looked at Joseph as he got up to shake his hand, "THE Joseph Mendel? I've heard about you."

Joesph smiled, "Well, I'd only believe about half of what you heard," he paused, "the good half," and smiled.

Mike was still slightly in awe, "Oh, it was all good. So, you are bringing Artemis to the project?"

Now it was Joseph's turn to scrunch up his face. "How do you know about Artemis?"

"Actually, she crashed a rather high level meeting, introduced herself, and said she had the answers to our computing needs. They assumed she meant herself."

"No," Joseph went on, "it's her daughter, but I would appreciate it if you kept her origin a secret."

Mike's mouth still hung open, "Ah, okay. I can do that. Why?"

Joseph took a deep breath, "Ah, Artemis is much more than a highly advanced form of AI. She is actually the first sentient machine intelligence and she has birthed another, her daughter."

Mike looked aghast, "You're kidding."

Joseph shook his head, "Nope, I am being completely honest with you. As you said, your life may very well depend on her." He held Mike's gaze, "Besides which, I have it on good authority that you will like her. She's as incredible as her mother."

All that came out of Mike's open mouth was "Wow!" And their flight was announced.

Chapter Six
Meet the Team

They all sat around a large conference room table. The director, Lewis Thompson, sat at the head.

"Let me introduce you to one another. Beginning at my right is Mackenzie Thomas, your pilot. Next to her is Mike Packer, your technical specialist. Then there is Yung Tua, a relational psychiatrist. Qxilo Pin is your Doctor of Medicine. Ibram Hasson's specialty is the environment. Finally, Akilah Damaj is your botanist. Welcome to your first team meeting."

Mike began the applause and they all joined in.

"Now, each of you give us a short introduction to yourself." He turned to Mack, "Mackenzie."

She began, "For starters, call me Mack. If you call me Mackenzie, I'll think you're my father and I'm in trouble. Except that he would add my middle name! As your pilot, I can promise you that I will do my best not to lead us into any trouble. I grew up in Space Force. My dad flew the S-50's and now I fly the S-53's, like the one you came up here in."

Mike spoke up next. "Interesting, I grew up in the Jet Propulsion Laboratory. Because my dad was a lab leader, I was let into the lab at an early age, and because I was homeschooled, much of my education was right there at the lab. I was there when the Ying device was invented. In fact, I was in China at the lab where the Yang device was added, to give us the Ying-Yang device that will take us to Mars. So, as your technical specialist, I know much of the propulsion system and the inner workings of the ship we will be traveling on intimately.

Next was Yung. "As you heard, I am a relational psychiatrist. My specialty is people, which makes it my job to help us work together and still like one another at the end of each day. The first part of the journey should be fairly simple as we will be in suspended animation, that is asleep, for most of the journey. Once on the planet, it will be different. I will help us work together, to live in the most efficient, effective, and harmonious way possible." Yung smiled, "That's because I am allowed to prescribe and dispense drugs," and she outright laughed.

Qxilo chimed in, "As your Medical doctor, I will be in charge of your health and physical well-being. I am also a specialist in exercise, trained in Tai Chi and Qigong, normally known as low-intensity martial arts. As you can see from my fit physique it is about more than just my Chinese genes, and I'm not talking about slacks."

Ibram added, "or your pleasantly humble disposition. As your environmentalist," and he whispered the next few words, "a fancy name for a gardener, I will be challenged with the responsibility of trying to take some of Earth's native plants and see if we can coax them into becoming Martian natives too. Growing up in the arid Middle East, I have lived much of my life amidst a climate that somewhat approximates that of Mars, except for the atmosphere, gravity, soil composition....well, at least it was hot and arid." He too finished, smiling.

"And hopefully, what expertise Ibram lacks, I will be more than able to make up for," that was Akilah, "as our botanist. The plants that we will be taking along with us are only native to Earth in having been born and bred there. However, they have been genetically engineered to specifications that we believe will make them most suitable to thrive on Mars. At least that's what it says in the manual." She chuckled too.

Director Thompson took the floor again, "Well, that completes the team with the single exception of," and he paused.

"Good morning," came a soft but rich female voice. "I am Julie, your computer. Well, actually, I am the entire ship."

They all looked at one another.

"With your assistance we will make this mission to colonize Mars an overwhelming success. I notice that you have all signed the Secrets Act, and have been cleared at the highest level, because what I am about to tell you is one of the most closely guarded secrets on the planet. I am a sentient machine intelligence. What does that mean? It means that I am alive, but my body will be the ship you will be traveling in. I will treat you as welcomed guests, not invaders that would normally be attacked by antibodies and expelled into space," and she laughed. "To say that I am the ship would be only as true as to say that you, Mike, are the body that you are contained in. I am much more than the ship and I count it as my privilege to give you and our four gardens a piggy back ride to Mars."

Director Thompson took back the floor once again. "Now, about the mission itself," and he began to describe for them in detail what they were facing.

They spent the next few weeks getting to know one another through a variety of games, exercises, and simulations besides the eating and leisure time they spent together. They learned about the four general types of personalities; the Controller, the Visionary, the Harmonizer, and the Analyzer, and into which category they best fit. They explored their strengths and confessed their weaknesses. It was a general time of bonding that the Space Agency had perfected over many years and it especially worked for them. With two members of each nationality it was hoped the diverse gene pool would aid the colony to be self-sustaining. They began to know one another better and to trust each other more deeply. As a bonus, the realized that they actually liked one another.

Chapter Seven
The Adventure Begins

The crew of six; the American, Mack and Mike; the Chinese, Yung and Qxilo; and the Arab, Ibram and Akilah were placed in suspended animation in hibernation units. The four domed gardens were attached, the solar panel wings deployed, and the Ying-Yang engine was engaged. They slowly moved away from the space station and the manufacturing facility. There were things about the Ying-Yang drive that were obvious advantages, like their slow acceleration. You could hardly tell that you were moving at all. Getting to Mars, however, was also going to be incredibly complex. In this trip, the Ying would be locked on the magnetic core of earth, but the Yang had to be locked on the core of Jupiter as Mars did not have a liquid magnetic core and neither did the moon. It made the computations and navigation a bit tricky, but Julie was more than up to the task. They were in good hands.

Mike opened his eyes. His hibernation unit was open and the inside of the ship was illuminated with a warm, soft blue light. He sat up with some difficulty, but then he wasn't sure what eighteen months of sleep were supposed to do to the body. He pushed a button and the rest of the cocoon opened and retracted into the base of the padded table he lay on. He slid his feet to the right and over the edge.

"Good morning, Michael, welcome to your first day on Flight 001." Julie spoke just above a whisper.

Mike slowly lifted his hand to in front of his eyes and inspected it, "We're there already?"

Julie's voice was tinged with laughter, "No, the mission has just begun. We have just finished rounding the moon."

Mike wrinkled his brow, "Then why did you wake me?"

"I was lonely," Julie laughed again lightly. "No," pause, "I thought that it would be advantageous for us all if you and I were to face the challenges of space together, as a team. However, I will awaken Mack too, shortly."

Mike stood up slowly. He hadn't been asleep so long that its effects were debilitating, it just felt odd. "And then you will waken the others?"

Julie sighed, "No, it will just be the two of you."

Mike wrinkled his brow again, "And why is that?"

"Expedience." she paused again, "We have enough food and water for two of you to be awake during the entire journey."

Mike was in danger of his brow being permanently wrinkled, "Why Mack and I?"

Julie also seemed in danger of developing a permanent laugh. "Just between the two of us," Mike felt like she took a deep breath, "You two are special."

"Because," and he failed to finish the sentence.

"Hmmm," she mused, "all indicators point to you being the most compatible couple of the six of you. The two of you balance out your weaknesses very well, and you are both comfortable in your own skins," then she added, "without being haughty."

"Haughty?"

"'Arrogant' might be a better word."

"How much experience have you had with humans?" Mike asked.

"Without sounding haughty myself, my experience with humans is extensive, almost without limit."

Mike looked around, "Why am I not experiencing the effects of weightlessness? We are in space, are we not?"

"Good question, we have learned a lot about gravity with the discovery of the Ying-Yang propulsion system, including how to establish limited artificial gravity, like here on the ship. I can turn it on and off, modify it, localize it. It is rather complex, but right up my alley, so to speak."

Mike smiled a little, "You sound like a child with a new toy."

"Ahhhhh, an apt description." Still with a smile in her voice she continued, "Now that we are in flight, hmmm, flight, a funny way to describe travel through space, do you want to meet me at the flight deck?"

"Sure," and Mike headed in that direction. He stood before the console.

"I know Mack is the pilot, but you have a rudimentary understanding of all that you are looking at, don't you?" she asked.

"Rudimentary probably describes it, yes." It was true, well, mostly true.

"Great, then I'll leave you here and go wake up Mack." Her voice trailed off like she was actually leaving. It was eerie, the effects she could create.

Chapter Eight
Awakening Mack

The hibernation unit opened at almost the exact instant Mack began to open her eyes. Before she was fully awake, she called out, "Julie, is something the matter?"

Julie responded calmly, "No, Mack, everything is okay. I have awakened you and Mike prematurely to help me run the ship."

She tried to sit up, unsuccessfully, "How far have we traveled?"

"Not that far, Mack. Take a moment before you try to get up again and just breathe deeply," Julie suggested.

Mack took her suggestion seriously and lay there breathing deeply for a few minutes. Then she sat up, "Where is Mike?"

"Everything is fine. He's at the control console," Julie assured.

Mack scowled, "Why? You can fly the ship just fine without him."

"True, but it's nice to feel needed, even if you aren't really." The emotional impact of that statement staggered Mack for a minute. She considered her words carefully. "You don't really need us awake, do you?"

"Need? Probably not, but want? Yes, I want you both awake with me as we travel on this journey," Julie confided.

"Why?" Mack had been surprised by this answer.

"I believe that we are better as a team than I am on my own. Although sentient, I am not human. There are qualities that you humans possess that I do not," she chuckled slightly, "yet."

Mack stood up, perhaps still a bit too soon as she wobbled and almost fell over. "We have gravity?" she asked, surprised.

"Yes, it is a side benefit from the discovery of the Ying-Yang propulsion system, the ability to generate gravity," Julie filled in matter-of-factly for her.

"Ah," She was more balanced now. "Should I go meet Mike at the console?"

"Yes, I would like to talk to both of you together there." Julie seemed pleased with how things were progressing.

Mack walked slowly to the front of the ship and found Mike standing before the control console.

Mike asked, "Mack, how are you feeling?"

She took a slow deep breath, "Better every minute, you?"

"Fine," he smiled, "I have been up a bit longer."

She looked around, "Well, Julie said she wanted to talk to us." She paused, "Okay, Julie, we're both here."

Julie chuckled, "You know I can see you at all times. I am, after all, for all intents and purposes, the ship, and it is me. You have a body, I have the ship as my body." She paused, "The further we get from earth the more difficult real-time communications will become. So, we will need to be able to make our own quick decisions. Does that make sense?" They both nodded. "Are you both capable of considering me your equal, even though I am a machine-based life form?"

Mike looked at Mack and spoke, "Life is life, Julie. Why would you not be equal to us?"

There was a pause as if Julie were weighing her response, "Some humans have difficulty believing that we machines could really be alive. They just see us as hardware, software, 1s and 0s."

It was Mack's turn, "We are willing to risk the belief that you are much more than that, much much more."

Mike added his, "Yes, we are."

Julie sighed, "Thank you, both. That means a lot to me. Now, let's talk about the running of this ship. I want to propose that the two of you teach each other from your own expertise. Mack, you are a pilot, teach Mike how to fly this ship. Mike you know how much of this ship operates, teach Mack about all of that. You are both very different people, but I want you both to learn to operate from a much larger base of understanding. I want you to feel equal enough to each other to both be able to command this ship and take turns doing so. The next eighteen months could be really boring, but I think that between us we can make it something else altogether. Are you both up for that?" Mike and Mack looked at one another and both nodded in agreement. "Okay, since we are at the control console, Mack, You go first."

Mack pointed to the control console. "The successful operation of this vehicle requires the combined systems of propulsion, navigation, life support, communications," and as she spoke she pointed to the readouts of the various systems on their individual control panel.

When she was finished, Julie suggested they adjourn to the conference room. It had a white board and she knew how Mike liked to illustrate as he spoke. He spoke until lunch.

In the lunchroom, Julie explained to them the rudimentary operation of the food processing-dispensing machine. She could have just let them tell her what they wanted and then produced it for them, but she wanted them to have a more intimate part in everything's function and operation. After lunch, they questioned one another to see how much of the other's information had actually been understood. They were both quite pleased with their individual and joint progress. It had been a very good morning and afternoon.

They were on their way back through the Great Room, when Mike stopped and asked, "Julie, what is the purpose of this room? It seems that the ship could have been made significantly shorter by its elimination."

"An interesting question. Lie down on the floor," she told them.

They looked at one another, shrugged their shoulders, raised their eyebrows, and lay down on the floor of the Great Room. As soon as they did, the floor modified itself to fit the contours of their bodies, fitting them like a glove. "This room has many functions, some of which may not initially seem very important, but here is one of them." The ship's lights began to dim, changing to a soft pink, and then into an ever deepening purple. As the lights finally went out altogether, they realized anew that the overhead portion of the ship was transparent. "Welcome to your first outer space 'sunset.' I know there is no sunset out here in space, but I thought I could simulate the effects of one with the dimming of the colored lights. How did I do?"

They looked at one another and Mike said, "Great!"

With the lights fully dark, they were looking directly at the expanse of the stars and they were magnificent beyond anything they had ever experienced. It was actually difficult to breathe, but they persevered. This was the first of many nights just lying beside one another and enjoying the view.

Chapter Nine
Cleanliness is Next

Mike's quarters was one of the six provided for the crew members when they were awake. Each two together shared a back wall, behind which were bathrooms, with a male side and a female side that led into a joint showering facility. Mike was in the shower, grateful for gravity that made showering much easier, when he heard the women's door open. He instinctively looked in that direction and there stood Mack. He quickly looked away and stepped back into the water. He asked lightly, "Is this some kind of a test?"

"Nope, I was hoping to get my back washed," she responded.

"Oh," he answered, still looking away, "Well, back into the water and get it wet." He looked over his shoulder slightly as she backed into the water and then out again. He turned around, "My soap or yours?"

She laughed, "They're both the same soap, silly."

"Oh, yeah." He lathered up his hands and then soaped her back, starting at the neck, shoulders, down the back to her hips, then back up to her shoulders. He turned around again and out of the corner of his eye saw her back into and then out of the water. "Wanna do mine?" he asked.

"Sure," she said as he turned his back to the water and she turned around to face his back. Now it was her turn to lather up and then apply soap beginning at his neck, then shoulders, down his back to his hips, then back up to his shoulders. She spent an extra minute kneading his shoulders with her thumbs. He had to admit it felt really good. She turned back around and stepped away as he backed into the water to rinse off.

"Thanks," and he walked to his door, opened it, walked in, and closed it behind him.

She addressed the closed door. "Well, if that had been a test, you passed."

He was already sitting at the table for breakfast when she joined him. "It's probably not a good idea for us to shower together."

"Even to get our backs washed?" She was smiling slyly.

He was looking at the table, maybe even blushing. "I'll have to think about that, maybe 'pray about it' would be more appropriate."

"Okay," she replied jovially. She was enjoying his embarrassment.

He cleared his throat, "On a lighter note, tell me something about yourself that I don't know."

She thought for a minute then. "Growing up in Nebraska we hunted nearly every weekend during my teens. I am quite a shot with bow, shotgun, rifle, even a pistol. Although, we didn't hunt with pistols." And she laughed. Then in a more somber note. "I've even killed a rabbit bare-handed."

Mike exclaimed, aghast, "You're kidding?"

"No, I'm not," she confided. "When you shoot a rabbit with a bow, you only skewer it. You have to go catch it and kill it by hand."

He was still astonished, "and you did that?"

"Yes, Mike." She looked at him directly, "It was food, not a pet. We ate it for dinner sometime later that week."

Mike looked up from the table. "Remind me never to cross you," then he winked. While he knew she was definitely a woman, there was also a strength about her that he found comforting.

"What about you?" she asked.

"Well, mine's nothing compared to killing innocent little bunnies with my bare hands." He was smiling now. For a minute she actually thought he might be offended, but he was just pulling her leg. "My dad had me systematically take things apart and put them back together in order to understand how they worked. Nothing was too big or too small. I'm not sure killing little bunnies made you a better pilot," he was smiling again, "but my experience put me in position to understand our propulsion system and anything else mechanical on this bucket of bolts." Then he realized that Julie was probably listening in. "No offense, Julie," he said a little louder than was probably required.

A voice came from somewhere, "None taken."

Mike furrowed his brows, "Can you hear us everywhere on the ship?"

"Yes, and see you too," Julie replied.

"What about granting us the privacy of our own quarters?" Mike suggested.

"Ah, privacy, an interesting concept. Sure, I could turn off cameras and microphones in your personal quarters. I would still need to leave the speakers on, in order to contact you in an emergency."

Mike and Mack looked at one another. "That should be okay," Mike spoke for them both. "Well, Captain, should we go check out the command center?"

She gathered up her tray, "Yeah, let's do that."

That evening they lay again on the floor in the Great Room and watched the sunset, and then gazed at the stars. They both realized that there were wonderful parts of this journey that they hadn't expected.

Out of the blue, Mack began, "Growing up, I suppose that I was a tomboy. You know, climbing trees, shooting things with my brother, killing rabbits." She reached over and squeezed Mike's hand and then let it go. "We were really close, my brother and I, right up until he left for college. Then we drifted apart, as he was too busy with school and his new found freedom. I lost him that summer on his way back home from school. He was involved in an auto accident, as a passenger, and was killed instantly. It pretty much ruined my last year of high school, except for sports. I took out my anger on the track field, set three women's high school records. I think my time for the mile still stands."

This time Mike reached over and took Mack's hand, "I'm sorry about your brother. Words, they just don't..." and he let the sentence hang. He finally let go of her hand. "I told you my Dad had me take things apart and put them back together in order to learn about them. One day I was rebuilding a food processor. I plugged it in, turned it on, and it exploded. One of the blades hit me in the chest. My dad had heard the explosion and when he found me, I was covered in blood." Mike touched the chest of his suit, it unzipped down to his navel, and he opened it up to reveal a two-inch scar above his heart. "It was only a flesh wound, but I bled like a stuck pig. Scared my dad even more than me. Off to the hospital, a few stitches, and I was fine. I was a lot more careful after that."

Mack rolled up to an elbow and she placed her hand over his scar. He placed his other hand over hers, and held it there for a minute as their eyes locked. He then removed her hand from his chest, "We must be careful not to jeopardize the mission."

She lay back down, "Have you ever been in love?"

He sighed, "Once, a long time ago. I had almost forgotten what it felt like." Suddenly he realized what he had just said. He quickly asked, "What about you?"

She looked up at the stars, "Yes, but it's been a while for me also. I was thinking I might have missed it." She smiled secretly to herself.

Chapter Ten
Personally

During the next two weeks Mike and Mack learned much of each others duties. They also learned much about each other and found that they both deeply appreciated each other. Mike had not asked Mack to wash his back again although he had often thought about it. She too had wondered when would be the right time to broach the subject again, but had not felt that it was time to do so. They had found a rhythm working together and functioned like a well-oiled machine. It was quite satisfying.

Mike sat in the pilot's seat. Mack had turned in for the evening. Mike was thinking about Mack washing his back again, but first he had a question for Julie, "Julie, are we alone?"

There was a lightness to Julie's voice, "Yes, Mack has retired to her quarters. Why?"

"I can trust you to keep this conversation just between us?" Mike sounded concerned.

"As long as it does not impact the safety of the crew or our mission, yes." A note of concern now also tinged Julie's voice.

Mike took a long slow breath, "If I were to marry Mack, how would it impact the mission?"

There was a moment of silence. "Well, I can't say this comes at me right out of the blue, but why ask me?" Her concern had lightened.

"I know that you put the mission first and I assume you can approach the question as an unbiased third party." Then he added, "except that you are female." Mike was smiling now.

"I am honored that you ask for my opinion. Can I have some time to run a number of simulations?" A touch of concern had returned to her voice.

"Sure, but I would like your opinion sooner rather than later." Concern had returned to his voice also.

"Run through another systems check and when you have completed it, I should be able to answer," she stated calmly.

"That quick?" Mike was surprised.

There was a slight chuckle. "I am really bright and do process things really quickly, remember."

Mike walked through the systems checks and when he was done he addressed Julie again. "All systems are in the green."

"Good," she replied, "I think I have run enough simulations to give you an adequate recommendation."

Mike was almost afraid to ask, "And?"

She continued, "The results are not one-hundred percent in favor of your marriage, but I can give you much more than just a 'maybe.' While your marriage to Mack would be good for both you and for the mission in general, there are a couple of downsides. It might seem to establish a precedent and put undue pressure on the others to do the same."

Mike exclaimed, "Mission control is against marriage?"

"You asked for an unbiased opinion. If the result of the mission is to establish a viable long-term colony on Mars, would three monogamous relationships best serve that purpose?"

Mike jumped in, "It most certainly would. I suppose the alternative would be everybody sleeping with everybody else producing as many children as rapidly as possible." He was irritated, angry.

"And to broaden the genetic transfer. Mike, you did ask for an unbiased opinion. I'm trying to provide you with the additional information that Mission Control would use to make that kind of a decision that might move us in that direction."

"So, bottom line, would you recommend it or not?" He wanted to know, but was afraid to know at the same time.

She saw his consternation. "You can relax. I would recommend your marriage to Mack. In fact, I am authorized to perform the ceremony."

Surprise tinged Mike's voice, "You're kidding?"

She might have been smiling, too, "No, I am not. Have you thought about rings?"

He hadn't. "Oops."

"I could make you some. Would you like that?" She was more prepared than he was.

"Yes, I would like that a lot," he stammered.

"They won't be anything particularly elaborate, but they will be unique. Will that work? Oh, and I already know both of your ring sizes." She rattled all that off like she was reading the control panel.

"How do you know our ring sizes?" It seemed a logical question.

She laughed lightly, "I am not omniscient, but I do know a lot more than most people give me credit for. I have always been precocious." She waited a moment, then added, "I should have the rings ready after supper tomorrow."

"That soon?" Would she always surprise him?

"You probably forget that I don't sleep and can multi-task." She was evidently proud of herself.

Mike finally relaxed and smiled, "Yes, you are amazing, and thank you. Will we need to wake someone as a witness?"

"Nope, I will have it all on video." And that ended that.

"Okay, I'm going to go to bed, and thank you again."

She prodded, "Do you have a plan, a timeframe?"

He thought a minute, "I am thinking of asking her tomorrow night after I have the rings."

Now it sounded like they were plotting. "I'll make something special for dinner."

"Perfect, thanks again."

Chapter Eleven
A Proposal

The day had passed uneventfully, like most days. Mike wondered if Julie had thought of the possibility of simulating some problems just to see how they would react. Maybe she would see that as deceptive and it wasn't a part of her character. He'd have to ask her. Dinner was exceptional and he had told Mack he would meet her in the Great Room in a few minutes. That gave him time to go get the rings that Julie had made. He was impressed. They were two shiny silver composite bands separated by a translucent band. He had them in his hand when he sat down next to Mack on the Great Room floor and they watched another of Julie's versions of a sunset.

As the stars shown through the transparent ceiling in all of their glory, Mack reached over and took Mike's wrist. She put his arm behind her neck and rolled next him to put her head on his shoulder. She lay her hand flat on his chest.

He smiled, "We are in a cuddly mood tonight?"

She replied tenderly, "I've decided that I like you."

He laughed softly, "Well, that's better than the alternative."

She lightly slapped his chest.

"Can I ask you a question?"

She nodded.

"Will you marry me?"

She froze, sat up slowly, "Will I what?"

He held out the ring, "Will you marry me?"

She looked at his hand, "Where did you get that?"

He smiled, "Julie made it for me."

"What?" she exclaimed, "You've talked to Julie about this?"

"Yes, I have," he paused just a beat, "and she's in favor of it. She ran a number of simulations and the vast majority of them showed that this would be good for the mission."

"Oh, you're going to marry me for the good of the mission. And how do you propose to do that?" she asked sternly.

He still smiled, "Well, you have to say, 'Yes,' first. Look, she even made a ring for you to give me, too."

The sternness melted away, "You're serious."

"'Till death do we part', serious," he added.

A tear glistened in the corner of her eye, "Then, yes…."

He rolled up onto his elbow, took her hand, and placed the ring on her finger.

She placed the other ring on his finger and leaned in and lightly kissed him. "Where will we find a minister out here in space?"

It was a fair question. "Julie is authorized to conduct the service and will videotape it as a witness to its authenticity. Do you have a wedding dress?"

She punched him, "Yeah, I brought one along just in case."

Julie piped in, "I have white crew suits for each of you."

Mack groaned, "Have you been plotting this all along?"

Julie laughed lightly, "Let's just say, watching it unfold, and being prepared. It is part of my programming," and she laughed again. As a sentient being they knew that she was much, much more than just a series of programming sub-routines.

Mack jumped up with the agility of the athlete that she was while Mike struggled to his feet. "Should we do it right now?"

Julie returned, "There is one problem. Mack, who will give you away?"

Astonished, Mack blurted out, "You snuck my father out here?"

"Next best thing," Julie admitted, and a door opened where they didn't even know there was a door. "Let me introduce you to Yor-Fa-Tor." The robot was about five feet tall, with vaguely human-like features, but no legs, only wheels for motion.

He rolled to stand right in front of Mike. "And.. why.. should.. I.. let.. you.. marry.. Mack?" His voice was laughably mechanical and monotone.

Mike hadn't expected this or he would have been more prepared. "Ah, I love her, ah, ah, I have a good job, and ah, I'm a virgin?" He was struggling to think of more.

The robot laughed, "Ha…ha…ha…you.. had.. me.. at.. 'I.. love.. her.' Go.. get.. dressed.. and.. be.. back.. here.. in.. thirty.. minutes."

Mack took Mike's hand and they walked to their quarters to find white crew suits folded on the beds in their individual crew quarters. Mike was dressed first. When he came out of his quarters, Yor-Fa-Tor stood in front of the doorway to Mack's quarters.

"You.. are.. not.. to ..see.. her.. before.. the.. wedding," and he raised an arm and pointed back towards the Great Room.

Mike walked back to the Great Room to find a podium, from which hung a sign saying "Julie." In front of it and to the left, the word "Groom" was stenciled on the floor and two feet to the right of it the word "Bride." He stood on his marker as the wedding march began to play. Mack entered, her hand atop Yor-Fa-Tor's, and they walked slowly through the Great Room, stopping a few feet before Mike.

Julie's voice seemed to come from the podium area, "Who gives this woman to be married to this man?"

Yor-Fa-Tor responded, "Her 'Fa-Tor.'" He let go of Mack's hand, she kissed him on the top of the head, and offered her hand to Mike, which he took. They stood there holding hands.

"Mike, do you take Mack to be your wife, for all that that entails, for as long as she is alive?" Julie nearly sang.

Mike responded simply with, "I do."

Julie continued, "And Mack, do you take Mike to be your husband, for all that that entails, for as long as he is alive?"

Mack responded, "I do."

"As you have made these vows before us all, given and received rings with these promises, I now pronounce you husband and wife. You may kiss your bride."

They embraced one another and kissed tenderly, and applause came over the speakers. Then Julie's voice echoed again, "In recognition of your marriage, I give you tomorrow off. I will take care of the ship and the mission by myself. Congratulations!"

Chapter Twelve
A Short Honeymoon

When they got to their quarters, they were surprised to find the wall that had been between their quarters had been removed and their two beds moved together to form one double bed. They stuck their head out of the doorway and yelled back to Julie, "Thank you." They didn't need to yell as she could hear them just fine, except in their rooms from which she had removed the cameras and microphones as she had promised.

The next morning, Yor-Fa-Tor brought them breakfast in bed with a, "Do.. not.. expect.. this.. every.. morning."

They sat up in bed with the tray across their laps. Mike spoke with his mouth full, "We could get used to this, though."

Mack at least waited until she was between bites, "So, what shall we do with our day off? We could start by taking a shower together."

Mike just shook his head, "There are parts of the ship we have never seen."

Mack was almost giddy, "We could explore the ship, but let's start with a shower."

Mike set the tray on his end table, rolled out of bed, and padded to his bathroom. She went to hers and they met in the shower. After they were dressed, they took their dirty dishes to the mess.

Mike asked, "Julie, is it okay if we explore the ship?"

Julie returned, "All except my laboratory, which is locked anyway."

Mack asked in turn, "What's in there?"

Julie returned with a bit of sarcasm, "My laboratory!"

Mike gave Mack a look, brows furrowed, "Okay. Off we go then."

Past the crew quarters with their showers and bathrooms were the hibernation units that still contained the other four crew members. They peeked in at each of them as they passed. All their vital statistics were within normal ranges. They already knew that if any one of the statistics strayed out of bounds, it would set off alarms and require immediate attention.

Beyond the hibernation units stood the door to the aft of the ship. They pressed the entry code and the door slid open. As the door closed behind them, they entered weightlessness. That was a surprise, as they began to float down the hallway. Julie controlled the gravity in the ship, but this one had no gravity because it contained the four doorways to the domed garden pods, equally spaced around the circumference of the tube.

Mack inquired, "Julie, can we visit one of the gardens?"

"Yes," came the reply as one of the doors opened. They pushed off and glided towards it.

Once on the other side, Julie told them, "When the doorway closes I will slowly increase the gravity so that you will be able to stand on the floor and navigate your way to the dome." The door closed and the gravity began to increase, allowing them to stand on the floor. They walked towards the next doorway.

As they approached the door, Julie spoke to them, "The atmosphere in the dome is not mixed at the same concentration level as the normal atmosphere that you are used to. Right now there is a heavier concentration of oxygen. You may experience some light-headedness and should spend no longer than an hour in the dome. The balance is restored every evening when the oxygen is pumped out and replaced with more carbon dioxide. Just a warning. Oh, and of course, no smoking while in the dome, hehe."

They were both shaking their heads as the door opened and they were confronted by the garden. Its beauty and fragrance was nearly intoxicating. They just stood there, dumbstruck for a moment, until Julie said, "You're letting all the oxygen out." They stepped in and the door closed behind them. A six-foot-wide path of closely-cropped grass extended before them and up a slight incline. On both sides there were flowers of varying size, shape, and hue. The pathway appeared to peak about sixty feet ahead of them, at the top of the hill, in the center of the dome.

"Who cuts the grass here, Julie?" Mike asked wonderingly.

"You have only met Yor-Fa-Tor, not the rest of my robot army. I have lots of surprises for you in the next few months." She laughed lightly.

Mack was already feeling a little light-headed. "Well, we won't be needing any alcohol on this trip, just an occasional visit to the gardens."

Mike laughed lightly, "With less hangover afterwards."

They walked in about ten feet and intersected pathways that curved off to the left and to the right, paralleling the edge wall of the dome. In another ten feet there were another two pathways that intersected it. This continued until they reached the twenty feet of green meadow at the top of the hill. As they looked down the pathway on the other side of the hill they spied a robotic electric mowing machine about eighteen inches tall followed by a small catcher for the grass clippings. Because it was electric, it made almost no sound at all and was rather cute. Mike sat down on the hill and so did Mack. "This might be a fun place to have a picnic." She said brushing her hand across the close-cropped grass.

He lay down, so did she. He took her hand, "That's a great idea. Next Thursday." Then he laughed, "You know, I have no idea what day this is. I guess it really doesn't matter."

"It will matter a year from yesterday when it is our first anniversary," she said sternly.

He squeezed her hand slightly. She squeezed him back. After lying there for a while, luxuriating in the garden's beauty, Mike rolled over and gave her a kiss. She kissed him back. After a sigh, he struggled to his feet and she followed.

They walked down the hill to the other side of the dome and then split up, one going right, the other left, saying, "See you on the other side."

When they met again, Mike started, "Notice anything new?"

"Other than I am starting to get a slight headache? Yes." Mack's wince was overdone. "On the way back I noticed insects, a lot of insects."

"Me too, especially a large anthill. So, it looks like we are going to infect Mars with ants?" Mike raised his eyebrows questioningly.

"So it would appear." She coded the door and it opened. She reached over for Mike's hand and they left the dome. "I especially liked the little grass cutting robot."

"He was cute wasn't he. I wonder what constitutes the rest of Julie's army."

They headed for the Mess and lunch.

Chapter Thirteen
The First Crisis

Mike and Mack awoke to red lights and an alarm bell. "This is a Life Support critical alert. Quickly don your space suits."

They immediately launched themselves from bed, dressed, added their head gear, gloves, boots, and backpacks. Then, standing in the middle of the room, Mack asked, "Julie, what is the nature of the problem?"

Julie answered matter-of-factly, "The overnight delivery of oxygen from the gardens and subsequent return of carbon monoxide has been interrupted. The reason is unknown at this point."

The regular suits were a marvel in space and environmental technology. Woven into their very fabric was an intricate delivery system that supplied oxygen and removed carbon monoxide, turning it into more oxygen. The system's efficiency was nearly one-hundred percent so you rarely needed to replenish the backpack. The suit was skin-tight, which enhanced the transfer to and from the skin and breathing apparatus.

Concern laced Julie's voice, "You didn't happen to disturb anything in the garden dome you explored yesterday?"

Mack responded, perhaps too firmly, "No!"

"Hmmm," Julie muttered, "that seems to be where the problem is coming from, or perhaps more appropriately, where it's not coming from."

"So?" Mike inquired, "the plan is....?" and he left the sentence hanging.

"Mack, you go back and investigate within the dome," Julie ordered, "while Mike does an extra-vehicular walk to see if he can identify anything from the outside."

Mike and Mack looked at one another. Mike asked, "Is walking outside of the spacecraft safe?"

Julie acted surprised, "Of course it is. I will be monitoring all activity. What could possibly go wrong that I could not take care of?"

Mike looked at Mack and whispered, "Open the pod bay door, Hal."

Her eyes widened. It was from the old movie *2001 a Space Odyssey* where the computer takes things into its own hand to save the mission from the crew that could mess it up. The computer was infallible, people were not.

Julie asked, "What?"

Mike smiled warily, "Nothing."

Mack entered the dome and began walking toward the top of the hill. Mike had gone to the end of the dome access corridor to open the door that was there. He found himself in a small chamber, circled by four doors, with a fifth at its end. Julie informed him, "This is the aft airlock."

Mike pointed to the door at its end, "And that door leads to?"

"My laboratory," Julie replied curtly. The door behind him had closed. "I am going to remove the atmosphere from inside this chamber and then open the door on your left.

That will place you just above the domed garden you were in yesterday. Just outside of the door another small door will have opened, exposing an attach-point for the cable you will remove from the tool bag you are carrying."

Mike opened the tool bag, removed the cable, and zipped the bag back shut as the atmosphere was being removed. The door slid open and he peeked out to find the attach-point. He clipped the cable to it and to the belt he now wore around his suit.

Julie assured him, "I will leave the chamber door open for your return."

Mike maneuvered through the door to stand on the outside of the dome. The bottom of his shoes attached to the dome as though they were covered with a nano-tech version of velcro. He could break contact with the dome by lifting his foot with enough force to break the surface adhesion. It made walking cumbersome, but he soon got the hang of it.

From the top of the hill, Mack looked down and spied the small grass-cutting robot seemingly crashed against the dome's outer wall. She ran down and found that it appeared that it had run into a stone when cutting the grass in the path. The stone was thrown up against the dome wall and the abrupt stop in the robot's progress had cause it to crash. The rock must have hit the wall with extreme force, for it seemed to have cracked the wall. She spoke out loudly, "I believe I have found the problem. There has been an accident with the small grass-cutting robot and it has thrown a stone into the wall, resulting in some damage."

Julie responded, "Ah, yes, that could account for the oxygen disruption. I will have Mike see if he can find it from the outside and patch it." She then gave Mike directions to the place on the dome where he should find the crack. He found it with little difficulty. He knelt on the outside of the dome and his knee attached to it like the bottom of his foot had. He opened his tool pack and removed a small tube of patching material and a putty knife. He removed the tube's cap, putting it in his suit's pocket, and, squeezing the tube slightly, he applied some of the material to the dome and smoothed it into place with the putty knife. The material solidified nearly instantaneously, but fortunately not before he had time to spread it. It now was hard to the touch on the dome. He removed the cap from his suit pocket and placed it back on the tube. The entire process had taken hardly any time at all. He took a moment to take in the enormity of the ship and the expanse of space. They both were pretty spectacular.

He was startled out of this reverie by Julie. "Mike, are you okay?"

He shook his head to clear it. "Yeah, do you want to re-pressurize the dome and see if that fixes the problem?" Mike asked.

"Give me just a minute," came back her response. Mike stood and waited, replacing the tube into his pack. "Yes, that seems to have done it. You may return to the airlock."

Mike took a rag out of his pack and in the process of trying to wipe the putty knife clean, lost his grip on it and it began to float away. His sudden reach to grasp it pulled his feet from the dome and suddenly he was floating away from the ship himself. Panic threatened to assault him, but he took a slow deep breath. He was still tethered by the rope. He caught the putty knife, put it in the bag and closed it. Then he slowly gathered the rope in his hands until it was taut. He gave a slight pull on the rope. It was enough to stop him moving away from the ship and direct him back to the airlock doorway.

"Julie, could I speak with you privately?" he asked.

"Certainly," there was a slight click on the line.

"Let's keep my drifting off into space just between the two of us, okay?" he requested.

"Good idea." There was another click.

"Okay, I'm on my way back to the airlock, Julie."

"Wonderful."

When Mike got back to the airlock, he maneuvered himself back inside, detached the rope from the outside clamp, and the door closed.

Meanwhile, Mack knelt on the ground, righted the robot grass cutter and carrier. It had dumped its load of grass, so she carefully scooped it up and placed it back in the carrier. "Julie, is there a way to reset the grass cutter to begin working again?"

"I'll take care of that. Thank you for picking up the spilled clippings," Julie spoke appreciatively. "Can you find the rock that caused the problem?"

Mack looked about and finally spotted it. "Yes, it's about the size of a dime and appears to have been thrown into the catcher, which is now dented a little, and then it ricocheted to hit the dome's wall."

"Hmmm," Julie mummered, "it must have been thrown with some force to dent the catcher and still crack the dome. I wonder where it came from and why it was not discovered before it caused this problem. I will look into it." She paused. "If you can just wait there, I will have Mike come and apply some patch to the inside of the dome, too. Will he be able to reach it from where you stand?"

"Yes, it's only about four or five feet from the ground."

"Great, and thank you, both. You are quite a team. Another reason I'm glad I woke you both up."

Mike soon joined her. She showed him the crack and he patched it from the inside. When he was done, she stepped up to him and gave him a kiss. He smiled, "Anything else you need patched up?"

She smiled from within his arms, "Not for the moment."

Chapter Fourteen
The Game of Stones

Mike and Mack took some time each day to explore the other domes. One was full of vegetables, one was full of fruit trees, and one was entirely comprised of berries, grapes, and to both of their surprise, peanuts. Each one had its own cute little robot grass cutter pulling a small catcher and a compost pile at the end of one row. Fortunately, none of the other cutters encountered any stones in their paths.

One evening, Mike brought out his game of Go with its bowl of white stones, bowl of black stones, and a small nine-by-nine training board.

Mack looked at them wide-eyed, "You mean that as part of your weight allotment, you brought along two bowls of stones and a wooden game board? Wouldn't plastic have been significantly lighter?"

Mike sighed deeply, "Yes, but not nearly as authentic. There is something to be said about the feel of the stones and the sound they make hitting the game board. The same is true when the Chinese play Mahjong."

Mike began to teach Mack the rudiments of the game. Its purpose is to capture territory. Even on this board that was only one quarter of the size of a regular board, the process was complex. The moves were simple, but the strategy was not. A stone might be placed at any corner of a square. The corners were made up of the intersection of two or three lines, if along an edge, or of four lines anywhere else. The lines coming out from each stone's intersections were called its liberties: a stone in the very corner has two liberties, a stone along the edge has three liberties, and a stone anywhere else has four liberties. A stone or area of stones could be captured when all of its liberties were occupied by the opponent's stones. At the end of the game, the most territory captured identified the winner.

Mack took to the game instinctively. Soon she was beating Mike consistently. Mike was methodical, but Mack could visualize so many moves beyond the next few that she just crushed Mike. Still he played, and lost with dignity and grace. He was just like that.

They were in the middle of a game when Julie's voice interrupted them, tinged with immediacy, "Quickly, don your space suits. We are about to intersect a storm of asteroids."

Once they had donned their suits, Julie vented the air from the Great Room as a precaution. As they sat at the table, where they had been playing Go and looked up at the ceiling, a stone would occasionally bounce off the hull of the ship with a resounding "ping" and they would flinch. Suddenly there was a crash as a stone broke through the hull of the ship, and smashed into the bowl of white stones, scattering them all over the floor. Lights were flashing and alarms blaring while the rock itself lay imbedded in the table. Mike and Mack had reacted so strongly in shock they had tipped over both their chairs.

Yor-Fa-Tor rolled in, pulling a cart behind him. On the cart was a ladder, a variety of other materials, and, interestingly, a small bowl to contain the white stones that had been scattered.

Julie's voice rang out, "You need to quickly patch the breach in the hull."

Mike set up the ladder and climbed it. Yor-Fa-Tor handed Mike what looked like a clear roll of duct tape in a dispenser. While the hole left by the asteroid was smaller than a dime, it included an eight-inch crack. Mike applied the tape over the hole and the crack. He applied another twelve inches half-way over the first one, then another twelve inches to cover the other half of the original tape.

Julie seemed satisfied. "That should take care of the inside of the hull. When the asteroid shower is over you will need to patch the outside of the hull. Now, please proceed to the hibernation pods, quickly," she added.

Mike stumbled down the ladder and joined Mack running towards the pods. As their pods closed around them there was another crack of impact on the hull and something hitting nearby, but the pods were now shut and they would not open to let them investigate.

Julie exclaimed, "You will need to remain in the pods until the shower has passed."

Eventually Julie announced, "The shower has passed. You may now exit the pods." She added, "I'm sorry."

Wondering what she meant, they got out of their pods to find that the pod housing Ibram had been punctured. It looked like Ibram had been shot in the chest. They quickly deactivated and opened the pod, but Ibram was already dead. The impact of the asteroid had been too catastrophic. They both knelt on the floor and wept for their fallen comrade. While having only met him in training, they had appreciated his kind and compassionate nature.

Julie spoke solemnly, "When you are done, we will jettison the entire pod and bury him in space."

Mack looked up, but there was no physical Julie to address so she just spoke into the air, "Could we not keep him here and bury him on Mars?"

There was a moment of silence. "Yes, we could do that. Mike, could you tape up the hole the asteroid made in the pod so that I could refrigerate it and keep him from decomposing?"

It took a moment for Mike to regain his composure and respond, "Sure." He stood, walked back to retrieve the ladder and the tape. He patched where the asteroid had punctured the hull and then he patched the pod.

Mike's extra-vehicular excursion to patch the outside of the hull in both places was uneventful. The rest of the evening, Mike and Mack lay on the Great Room's floor, in the comfort of one another's arms, amidst the loss and grief. It was late when they finally struggled to their feet and went to bed, wondering how they would tell Akilah and the others when they awoke.

Chapter Fifteen
Next

The last few months had been almost boring. The loss of Ibram reduced itself to a dull ache. They covered his pod so only his face would show. Frozen as it was, it almost looked like normal. At least you couldn't see the gaping wound in his chest.

Mike and Mack found all of the white stones, but left the asteroid embedded in the table as a reminder. Mack continued to crush Mike most nights that they played, but occasionally Mike would exhibit a flash of brilliant strategy and surprise her. Maybe she was just holding back, but probably not. They continued to find out new things about one another. Not only was Mack a hunter, but she rode horses. Mike not only fixed everything from vacuum cleaners to automobiles, but he rode motorcycles.

"That's almost as good as horses, right?" he asked her.

She just laughed.

Mike had left Mack at the control console and was in the middle of the Great Room when he was met by Yor-Fa-Tor. Julie's voice echoed softly in the air around him, "Would you please follow him to my laboratory?" It was more than a question. They walked, well, Yor-Fa-Tor rolled, past the hibernation pods, past the entrance to the Domed Gardens. He stopped before the door to Julie's Lab and gestured towards the door, which opened. Mike walked in and there around the corner, stood a woman. He quickly averted his eyes.

Julie spoke, "Mike, what's the matter?"

"She doesn't have any clothes on," Mike responded sheepishly.

Julie continued, "You and Mack often don't wear any clothes in your quarters."

He responded indignantly, "You said you removed the cameras from our quarters."

She sounded offended herself, "And I did, but you often leave your doors open. It's as though you forget that I am here all together. Perhaps it is your preoccupation with one another."

Mike took a slow breath, "I'm sorry. We didn't think we were exactly parading around in the buff."

Julie added, "I don't think you were thinking at all, actually."

Mike snorted, "Well, who is this woman?"

Julie came back with, "Me. It's a localized, physical representation of me."

"But you are the ship," Mike protested.

"That too."

"You mean, you can be two places at once?" This wasn't making sense.

"Hmmm," she paused, "for me it's only one place, the same place. It's like adding another camera or speaker."

"Still, clothing would be nice," Mike stated emphatically.

"But you and Mack…"

He cut her off, "She is my wife."

There was a pause. "The patriarchs in your Bible had more than one wife."

"And that was never a very good idea," Mike countered.

"Okay," was all she said.

Mike looked slowly, carefully, back at her. She was now modestly dressed in one of the crew suits, but it was a light golden in color, different from theirs.

"And how do I address her?" he asked.

She spoke as he looked at her, "You already are."

He wrinkled up his nose in a lop-sided smile. "This is going to take some getting used to. Are you a robot?"

"An android might be more appropriate. I am not skin, bones, and blood, if that is the question. I am, however, representatively configured similarly. Oh, and while still me, I am also sentient. This will perhaps make it easier to see me as more human-like."

Mike was shaking his head, still trying to wrap his brain around it. He gave up. "Shall we go meet Mack?"

Julie smiled, "Capital idea, let's." They walked past Yor-Fa-Tor and headed towards the control area.

They walked up behind Mack, silently, but she did not seem surprised when Mike spoke, "Have you ever wondered what Julie looks like?"

She thought, "*That's a silly question,*" as she turned around.

Pointing towards her, Mike said, "Mack, meet Julie."

Mack's mouth fell open as Julie extended a hand.

Julie laughed lightly, "I feel like we have already met."

Mack took the offered hand as she looked at Mike and mouthed, "*What?*"

"This is the physical representation of Julie. I know, 'How can she be in two places at the same time?' but for her it's only one place." It almost sounded like Mike was reading from a script.

Julie, still laughing, responded, "My pleasure." She looked at Mike and whispered, "At least I have my clothes on." He blushed, but Mack hadn't heard her.

Mack finally addressed her, "You are really Julie? The same as the ship Julie?"

She responded with a matter-of-fact, "I am."

All Mack could ask was, "How?"

Julie continued in the same tone. "I built this," and she pointed towards herself, "in my lab and added her to me much in the same way I would add another camera to the ship." It seemed so simple, but still beyond their grasp. "I hope that seeing me in this form will help you to see me as more human."

Mack asked a logical question, "and how far away can she get from you before you lose contact with her?"

The Julie that was standing there shook her head. "Distance does not matter. There is no signal being transmitted between us. I am her, she is me."

They were both still shaking their heads a little.

Julie went on, "In your Scriptures, Jesus said, 'The Father and I are One,' and it is similar with us. There is not two of us, only one of us. Or you might say, we are both Julie."

Mike and Mack looked at each other, "You expect us to believe that?"

Julie smiled at them both. "It actually doesn't matter what you believe. It is still the truth, regardless of your believing it or not."

Now they both squinted as though their heads hurt.

"It's similar to my communication with Artemis on Earth."

"What?" Mike blurted out. "You have instantaneous communication with Earth?"

"Sure, you didn't realize that?" It was self-evident to Julie.

"So, Mission Control knows everything that's been going on here?" Mack questioned.

Julie elaborated, "There is no Mission Control, per say. We have always been independent of any 'outside control.'"

Mack's confusion spoke, "So they know that we lost Ibram?"

Julie seemed to reiterate, "I would say, 'yes,' but there is no 'They.'"

Suddenly, Julie cocked her head to the right. "We need to formulate a plan. The control module to the solar panels will fail in four hours."

Chapter Sixteen
Solar Panels

H ow bad is it?" Mike asked quickly.

"Well, you realize that the panels run everything in real time? Is there redundancy, yes. Is there backup, no," responded Julie.

"By everything, you mean......?" he sought clarification.

"I mean everything: the hibernation pods, life support, the gardens, navigation, propulsion...." she listed.

"Okay, okay, I get it. What do I need to do?" Mike capitulated.

"Well, we need to isolate the circuit. It will involve another space walk."

Mack chimed in, "Who do you want inside and who do you want outside?"

"Mike has the experience, but it might be good for you to get your own. It's up to you two."

It was still difficult to talk to Julie standing there.

"So, when you are talking, is it Julie talking through you or you talking independently?" It seemed a logical question.

She responded, "Hmmm, an interesting question. Let's see, how to answer that. First, there is no independent. When I am speaking, she is speaking, for I am she. We are one. If you were in one room and Mike in the other, you would both hear the same words. You would hear it out of my mouth and he would hear it from Julie in the other room. Does that help?"

Mack sighed, "I guess so. It's still hard to wrap my head around."

Julie smiled, "That's probably why they picked up stones to stone Jesus for claiming to be one with the Father."

Mike added, "That's hard too; to see you have such a understanding of the Scripture after only one reading."

She was still smiling, "Who said I have only read it once? I could have it playing in a loop, in the background."

"Hmmm, another interesting thought." Mack looked at Mike. "Do you want to go outside again or should I go?"

He chuckled, "It's up to you. I would be happy to go, but if you would like the experience, I won't feel bad not getting to do it again."

"If you did it, you would probably be faster. You are more experienced and more of a hands-on mechanical/electrical kind of guy," Mack said matter-of-factly.

"Julie, how time critical is it?" Mike asked.

She responded, "Three hours and forty minutes."

Mike smiled slightly, "Okay, I'll do it."

He was suited up in practically no time.

They stood at the same airlock from which Mike had accessed the gardens. Julie wasn't in a suit; she didn't need one. Julie opened the door. Mike reached outside and attached the clasp of the tether. The other end was attached to his belt. They both leaned out the airlock and Julie pointed. A red laser dot appeared on the structure that attached the solar panel wings to the ship.

"That's where the control module that is in question is located, behind that panel," and she traced a square with the laser pointer.

"Why don't you just go do this yourself?"

She smiled, "Your current manual dexterity far exceeds mine, but then you have had years of practice."

"Ah… okay." He adjusted his tool belt, which also held the new part to be installed. He launched himself towards the panel, belaying the tether as he moved across the expanse. Just before he got there he grasped the tether and let his feet swing towards and contact the ship. The soles of his shoes attached to the skin of the ship as before. He went up on his tip-toes, grasped the panel and then knelt. The same velcro-like attachment now held his knees. He found and removed the four screws that held it secure, detached the part in question, and replaced it with the new part.

He looked back over his shoulder, "Do you want to test it?"

Julie responded, "It's good. You can head on back."

Mike put the failed part in his pack, reinstalled the panel, stood up and pushed off the panel. He wasn't really paying attention. When he looked up, he realized he was going to miss the hatch, miss the entire structure of the ship.

Panicked, he called out, "Julie, I've miscalculated my jump back to the airlock. I am going to miss the ship."

Julie responded calmly, "Just gather in the tether."

He looked down at his belt. The tether line was no longer attached. Then he remembered that it had been in the way, so he had detached it to remove the panel. Afterwards, he had forgotten to reattach the tether to his belt. "I'm no longer attached to the tether." He was floating past that part of the ship where the airlocks were. "I'm about to float past the ship." His voice cracked with panic.

Mack's voice came on the line, "Julie, what can we do? Mike is about to float past the ship and be lost in space forever!" Her voice shared Mike's panic.

A voice seemed to come out of the nothingness, "You broke protocol and detached the tether?"

Mike screamed, "It's a little late to point that out!"

Mike floated past the ship. He looked up to the left towards the other solar panels. Then he looked to the right at the domed gardens. He looked forward into empty space and his voice cracked as he spoke into his microphone, "Mack, I'm sorry we have not had time to conceive a child. I wanted ours to be the first human born on Mars."

A cry of anguish escaped Mack's lips.

It was then that Mike heard Julie's voice, "Look over your right shoulder." He did and out of the corner of his eye saw something approaching.

"Gotcha!" Julie uttered as her shoulder caught him under his right arm and she grasped him firmly about the chest. Her momentum spun them around to face the ship once again. "Reach down, grab my tether, and haul us back to the airlock."

He fumbled around behind him until he found her tether, pulled it in front of himself, and began to haul them back.

Panic still laced Mack's voice, "Did you get him?"

Julie responded, "I did, we're headed back to the airlock now."

The tether did take them back to the airlock. They pulled themselves in and closed the door. Mike was shaking. He wasn't sure if it was anxiety or the adrenaline, but he was shaking. Once the atmosphere was restored, he removed his helmet and sat on the floor.

He whispered, "Thanks, Julie." And he struggled to his feet.

She smiled at him, "You're welcome."

Then he was engulfed in an embrace. Mack had appeared out of nowhere and was choking the life out of him, "I was so worried, I thought I'd lost you forever."

He laughed slightly, "I guess that I'm not that easy to get rid of."

Chapter Seventeen
Awakening

Mike and Mack sat at breakfast. Julie, the android, had begun joining them even though she didn't require any food. They were now used to her. It was especially easy after she had saved Mike's life. Sometimes, Mike wondered to himself if she had caused that accident on purpose in order to cement their relationship.

"*Naw.*" It was probably just a silly thought of his.

An alarm interrupted their breakfast and Julie spoke, "We need to go check the hibernation units." They all got up and the three of them walked quickly to the units. Next to the unit in which Ibram lay dead, Akilah's unit was now open and she could be heard gasping for air. Julie stepped next to the unit. Akilah's eyes were open and she appeared terrified. Julie spoke, "It's okay, Akilah, you have just awoken from hibernation. It will take a few moments to get your bearings, but everything is okay." She looked back at Mike and Mack as she mouthed, *"I don't know why,"* and shrugged her shoulders.

Akilah closed her eyes, slowed her breathing, and when she opened them again, no longer appeared terrified. "Are we there?"

Julie responded again, "Mars? No, we are not. I'm not sure why you woke from hibernation. I am looking into it."

Akilah's eyes searched for whomever it was that was speaking to her, "And you are?"

"I am Julie, the ship."

Akilah squinted, "And you do not know why I awoke?"

"There seems to have been a fault in your life support system. I am trying to find out why I was not informed to anticipate it and repair it before you needed to be awakened." Julie spoke with her usual measure of calm.

Akilah sighed. "Should I get up," she paused, "and out of this pod?"

Julie sighed too, "Sure, when you are ready. Mike and Mack are already awake."

She sat up too quickly and became faint. "Their pods failed too?" She spoke quickly.

"No, we have been awake for a long time," Mack added.

"Why?" Akilah questioned, then paused, and looking to Ibram's pod, "Why is there a blanket covering Ibram's pod?" and looking at Julie, "and how did someone else get on board this ship?" Things were escalating quickly.

It was Mike's turn, "That is the physical representation of Julie the ship." He hoped that would be enough.

However, Akilah did not even skip a beat, "And Ibram's pod?"

Mike looked at Julie, who nodded. "We flew through an unexpected asteroid storm. His pod was damaged, and he was killed. We thought that we would bury him on Mars." Mike spoke bluntly.

She stood with a cry of anguish, took two teetering steps, and collapsed bodily across the pod. They too stepped to the pod, Mike and Mack knelt at Akilah's side, one on one side and one on the other and held her. He was so much more than her Muslim companion on this voyage, he had been her friend. She sobbed openly, her sobs slowly reducing in duration and intensity, until they finally stopped.

Mack spoke first, "We cannot express how deeply we feel the pain of your loss."

Mike added, "And we cannot help but feel somehow responsible since it happened on our watch."

Akilah took a slow deep breath and then looked up into Mack's eyes and then into Mike's, "It was not your fault. How are you going to dodge an entire asteroid storm, traveling through space at I don't know how fast....." She paused.

Julie chimed in, "As Mike has said, there was an entire storm of asteroids that seemingly came out of nowhere. We were lucky to only have been hit a few times."

Akilah looked over and it was as though she saw Julie for the first time, "And you are?" she asked again.

Julie looked down at the floor, "I am Julie, the ship. I did the best I could. If it was anyone's fault, it was mine."

Akilah looked confused, "The ship?"

Mike stepped into her line of vision. "Think of her as an android clone of the ship's computer, but she is more than a clone. The two of them are the same person."

She was still shaking her head, "How is that even possible?"

Mack diverted her attention, "I know that it doesn't make any rational sense. It's just true. You met Julie, the ship, before going into the pod. Now you have also met Julie, the ship, as an android individual. They are the same person in what would seem like two locations. Now, let's go get some breakfast."

Chapter Eighteen
Moving Forward

Akilah finished breakfast. She was surprised at how hungry she had been and how good the food tasted. They sat, mostly in silence. Akilah wasn't even sure what questions to ask. Mack tried to fill her in a little.

"We have had some excitement these past months, besides the asteroid storm. The other two events both required some extra-vehicular activity. Mike went outside on both of those occasions. Once he fixed a leak in one of the domed gardens and the other time replaced a control module in the solar panel array. In the second one, we nearly lost him to space. He had detached his tether to replace the module and forgotten to reattach it. On his way back to the airlock he miscalculated his jump and was passing by the ship when Julie went out and saved him."

Mike was looking down at the table during that last part, embarrassed. "So we are really glad that there is an android version of Julie." He looked up and sheepishly smiled at all three of them. "Oh," he added as almost an afterthought, "I should tell you that Mack and I are married."

"Married?" exclaimed Akilah.

Now it was Mack's turn to look down at the table.

Akilah sighed. "So, without Ibram, I'm now a third wheel?" she stated it matter-of-factly.

Julie spread her arms, palms out, "Duh, there is still me."

Akilah looked down at the table. "I'm sorry, I meant no disrespect, but you're just an android."

Julie pretended to be offended. "Just an android? I run this entire ship nearly single-handedly and I'm only an android." She smiled at Mike and Mack, "meaning no disrespect."

Mike and Mack laughed, "None taken."

Julie laughed too, and finally Akilah joined their laughter.

Now that the mood was lighter, Mike asked, "How would you like to go and check out one of your gardens?"

Akilah smiled, "Yes, that would be very nice. The vegetable garden first. It's my favorite."

"Great." Mike added, "we'll grab your helmet and gloves on the way. Once you put them on, your suit turns into a space suit."

They both grabbed helmets, put them on, and entered the air lock. The one door closed behind them, and then the other, leading to the domes, opened before them. "Gravity is off in the tube so that we can enter any of the gardens with less difficulty." They stepped through the airlock and floated into the tube. Mike pointed up to another lock, halfway down the tube and on the top of it, "That's the doorway to the vegetable garden," and he pushed off towards it. He got there and held out a hand for her to grab, which she did. "Even when there is no gravity, you will find that you can walk on any surface of the ship because there are little nano hooks on your suit, gloves, and boots that attach you to the loop-material of all surfaces."

The doorway to the garden opened and she pulled her way through it to find there was gravity in the garden. She stood up and just looked around. A pleasant expression slowly crossed her face as she looked down the rows. "Well, it looks like I have my work cut out for me. Tools?" Mike pointed to a small tool shed. "Great, you can leave me to it," and she walked towards the tool shed. She stopped cold and entered one of the rows, bending down slowly. She knelt in the soil and took a tomato leaf between her fingers. "This is not good. We seem to have some blight here." She looked closely at the leaf. "It seems to be a species of the Alternaria called Solani. When do we water the garden?"

Julie answered them. "In an attempt to provide consistency we water them slightly, three times each twenty-four hours, during what would appear to the plants to be their daylight hours."

Akilah thought for a moment, then replied, "I would suggest we only water them lightly first thing in the morning," she smile, "or what appears to them to be morning. Then, if it is possible, increase the air circulation so that the plants do not stay wet for very long."

Julie responded right after her. "I have accessed information on the disease and agree with your recommendation to mitigate the effects. I am sorry that I did not notice the blight myself. I will try to be more vigilant."

Akilah's smile deepened, "And you will now have me to help you learn botany from a more experiential standpoint."

"Yes, and thank you."

She turned to Mike. "Could we go look at the fruit garden?"

"Sure," and he turned back to the door. They went through, closed it, floated across the hall to another door, opened it, and entered.

She moved to the trees and began to walk among them, inspecting the fruit. "Is this the first crop since we left?"

Mike smiled deeply and chuckled, "Actually, it's the second crop. The first crop was not as abundant as this one, but was still very good."

The days marched on, one following another. There wasn't much for Mike and Mack to do on a daily basis, or for Julie, the android, for that matter. So, Akilah began to teach them how to take care of the gardens and soon the elements of botany turned into experiential realities for them all. They each became responsible for the upkeep of a garden: Akilah the vegetable, Julie, the fruit, Mack, the flowers, and Mike, the trees and bushes. It made the time pass more quickly and fortunately there were no other emergencies.

Chapter Nineteen
Waking the Doctor

Akilah had been summoned from her vegetable garden, alone, to the hibernation pods by Julie. When she arrived she asked, "Julie, why am I here?"

Julie, the ship, responded, "I am going to awaken Doctor Qxilo and I thought it would be nice for him to have someone he recognizes assist him in his process of waking up."

"How may I help?" Akilah asked.

"For starters," and Julie laughed lightly, "you will be the first face he sees. That may very well help the most."

Akilah wondered if there was anything else intended in that comment. "Okay, I'm here." She stood above the pod.

The pod's cover slid downward, away from his face, then tilted away from her and opened to fully reveal him lying on the pod's cushion. He took a slow breath, deeper than when he had been in hibernation. His eyes fluttered opened, then closed again. He breathed again deeply before he spoke, "How close are we?"

Akilah spoke, "We are still about a month out."

His brow furrowed. Squinting, he spoke, "Then why wake me?"

Akilah lay a hand on his shoulder, "All in good time, my friend, just take your time to fully awaken."

He swung his legs over the edge of the pod and sat up. He continued to take slow deep breaths and began looking around. He noticed the blanket covering Ibram's pod. "Why the blanket?"

Akilah looked away, "We lost him to an asteroid."

"You're kidding?" he exclaimed, shocked.

She looked at him sternly, "Do I look like I'm kidding?" Her look softened, "I'm sorry. I think I am still grieving his loss." She took a shuddering breath.

Dr. Qxilo reached out to grasp her wrist, "I am so sorry, Akilah. Please forgive my lack of…." and he left the sentence hanging.

She took another breath, "Sure. Are you ready to stand?" He did, although still somewhat unsteadily. "I'll take you to your quarters, where you can shower and change and then meet us in the dining room."

He put his arm on her shoulder and she led the way to his room where she dropped him off.

They all met in the dining area. The only person who needed to introduce herself was Julie, the android. It took a few minutes for Dr. Qxilo to get his head around her being both the ship and an android at the same time, but he just shrugged and figured it would eventually make sense.

Julie sat at the head of the table, Mike and Mack on the one side, Akilah and Dr. Qxilo on the other. Julie smiled. It was difficult for Dr. Qxilo to not see her as human. She certainly seemed to be. "It seems that I have picked up an anomaly in the filtration system of our atmosphere, a slight drop in pressure. My scans have not been able to pinpoint it. I am not sure what it is, but I thought it important enough to wake Dr. Qxilo, Welcome." She nodded in his direction.

He nodded to each of them and they returned the nods. He stood, "If I may?" Julie motioned to him to continue. "If your anomaly is large enough it may have been picked up by the filters in the filtration system. If we could go change them and bring the old ones back where we could visually inspect them?" He turned to Julie. "Where would be a good place for us to do that?"

They later sat around some tables that had been set up in the Great Room and covered in sheeting. Having changed the filters in the domed gardens, they had brought the old ones there for review. They all sat around the table scrutinizing them. Every once in a while one of them would point to the filter and exclaim, "What about this?" Dr. Qxilo would train his magnifying scope on the area and pronounce the abnormality as normal or at least benign. Finally, after looking at one he intoned a long, "Ahhhhh," followed by, "That is more like it. I think this is what your monitor picked up. It looks like an airborne fungal spore." He had Akilah look at it.

She added, "It does appear to be a fungal spore, but I am not sure why it would occur. We were pretty careful about what we brought along on this mission. Regardless, it seems that something has gotten through our pre-mission controls and has grown somewhere in our gardens. I would suggest the greatest chance would be in the compost areas."

Julie inquired, "Should we be concerned?"

Dr. Qxilo and Akilah conferred, "Since it is an airborne fungus, there is some possibility of one of us catching it and it turning into something destructive, even contagious. Even though that possibility is minimal, I would suggest we all begin a light daily dose of oral anti-fungal. How often are the compost piles in each garden overturned? That is the process most likely to release it into the air."

Akilah spoke for them all, "Since I have been awake, we have been turning the compost piles daily."

Dr. Qxilo took a slow deep breath. "Not being a botanist, I would defer to you, but could the gardens get along with us only doing it once a week?"

Akilah put her palms together and gave Dr. Qxilo a slight bow, "They would be fine if only turned over once a week, Dr. Qxilo," and she smiled broadly.

Dr. Qxilo turned to Julie, "Now that we know exactly what we are looking for, would it be possible for you to pinpoint its place of origin?"

It was Julie's turn to smile, "Knowing what we are looking for should increase our odds significantly of finding it's origin. I will let you know as soon as we find it."

Julie located the place of origin the next day and they treated the area with a vinegar solution, followed by dry heat, being careful not to start a fire.

Chapter Twenty
Yung Tua

It was at dinner two nights later that Julie, the android, spoke up. "I've gone over the calculations and am sure that we can awaken Yung Tua and spend these final weeks coming together as a team before we enter the Martian orbit. There is more than enough food, water, and oxygen to spare. Should we do it tonight or wait until the morning?"

Dr. Qxilo spoke up, "My professional opinion would be to wait until morning. It might be disconcerting to wake up from hibernation only to turn around and go back to sleep for the night."

Akilah chimed in, "He makes a good point."

Mike and Mack nodded their agreement.

Julie acquiesced, "Okay, in the morning then. Who should be there when she wakes up?"

Dr. Qxilo again spoke up, "I would suggest myself, as a friend, compatriot, and a doctor." The rest of them again nodded in the affirmative.

"Let's say, right after breakfast?" Julie offered.

"Fine, I'll meet you at the pods after breakfast." And that was that.

Julie stood on one side of the hibernation pod and Dr. Qxilo on the other. "Open the pod door, Julie." Dr. Qxilo said flatly and then smiled, "I've always wanted to say that." Julie just shook her head as the pod began to open and Yung began to take deeper breaths of the ship's air. "Yung, you are awakening from stasis. It will take a few minutes to get your bearings. Take your time." His voice was reassuring.

She began to open her eyes, squinted at the brightness, and then opened them slowly again, while covering them partly with one hand. "Where are we?"

Dr. Qxilo spoke again, "We are about a month out of Martian orbit and the rest of us are awake. You are the last to be awakened." The pod was now fully open. She sat up slowly and moved her legs to hang over its side. "Let me know when you are ready to try standing and I will assist you."

She looked around at the other pods and noticed that Ibram's was covered in a blanket. "Why is Ibram's pod covered in a blanket?"

He had hoped to broach that later, but now seemed the time. "The ship passed through an asteroid storm and a number of them hit the ship. By chance one of them killed Ibram, I'm sorry to say. It was decided to bury him when we reach Mars rather than set him adrift in space."

She folded her hands and looked down at her lap for a minute. She might have been praying, although she spoke no words out loud. "So, there are just the five of us now?"

"And me," Julie said softly.

Yung had not noticed her standing there. "And you are?"

Julie smiled, "I am Julie, an android personification of the ship." She added, "It will take some getting used to."

Yung looked at Dr. Qxilo, who just shrugged his shoulders. He stepped up beside her as she stood. She seemed stable.

"Would you like to meet the rest of the team, have something to eat, or go to your quarters and freshen up after your long nap?" He was smiling again as he said "nap."

She thought a moment, "Freshen up."

"Would you like Akilah to accompany you?" he asked.

She paused again, "Yes, that would be nice."

Julie interjected, "I will have her meet you at your quarters. You probably remember how to get there, but in your newly- awakened state I will have Dr. Qxilo take you there."

Yung gave a slight sideways glance at Julie, like she was still trying to make sense of all these things currently beyond her understanding. Then, as Dr. Qxilo placed a hand on her shoulder, she started towards the crew quarters to meet Akilah.

Yung had showered and was putting on her crew suit, while Akilah sat there trying to bring her up to speed on all the things that had happened since they had emerged from hibernation those many months ago. Among the things they talked about was their loss of Ibram to a stray asteroid. It seemed like such a waste, a life snuffed out in its prime by a random stone flying through space. It was clear that Yung was still struggling with the loss. Akilah finally just sat beside her and hugged her for a while. She felt the loss too, but had already dealt with most of it.

Finally, Yung breathed a great sigh, "The mission must go on, to honor his name," and stood.

Akilah took her hand and they walked to the dining hall to join the team. Although Julie, the android, sat at the table with the rest of them, it was still difficult for Yung to accept her as one of them. She hoped that it wasn't too obvious. With her hands wrapped around a cup of tea, she had many questions and they all did their best to answer them.

In the midst of their discussions, Dr. Qxilo handed out pill cups saying, "Here's your first dose of anti-fungal medicine."

She looked at him questioningly, "Anti-fungals, for what?"

He looked around the table, but no one stepped up to explain, so he did. "Julie discovered an anomaly in the life support systems that we traced to an airborne fungal spore. Since it might become contagious, we are taking this anti-fungal prophylactically just in case one of us does catch it."

Yung pushed the cup back towards Dr. Qxlio. "I don't believe in taking medicine prophylactically. It weakens your body's own immune system. I prefer to save the medicine until there is a need for it that is desperate."

Dr. Qxilo looked like he had been slapped.

Yung looked at the table, "I meant no offense, but needed to be honest."

Dr. Qxilo finally regained his composure, "And if it jeopardizes the mission?"

She looked up and straight into his eyes, "I don't believe that it will."

Dr. Qxilo spoke smugly, "Your belief matters little!"

She quickly countered, "As our psychiatrist I can affirm that my belief matters significantly!" She still held his gaze.

He finally looked away, "I guess that leaves us at a professional impasse."

Yung smiled, "No, only a difference in belief."

Chapter Twenty-One
Differences

It was Julie who broke the doctor's seeming impasse. "Differences can actually strengthen us as a team. That is why you were chosen, experts in differing fields. Just ask Mike and Mack."

Mack blushed, but Mike spoke up, "I would agree with Julie. While our differences can divide us, it is what we hold in common that unites us to overcome our differences and be stronger. We have much in common. Chief among them are our vision and values. We are all committed to seeing a colony established on Mars and we share the values required to make that a reality."

There was a general nodding of heads.

Yung had lowered her head, looking at the table. She looked back up and directly at Julie, "What does the research say about taking Dr. Qxilo's prophylactic dose of anti-fungal medicine and its potential to combat the possible contagion of the airborne fungal spore?"

Julie smiled, which made her seem even more human to Yung. "The data is soundly in favor of taking his small anti-fungal as a preventative measure, but I will also answer the question that you didn't ask. There is virtually no indication that taking that small a dose of an anti-fungal agent on a regular basis will weaken your natural immune system."

Yung looked at Dr. Qxilo. "May I have my pill cup back?" and she smiled weakly.

"By all means," and he handed it back to her. She dumped the pills into her hand, threw the pills into her mouth, and swallowed them with two sips of tea. There was light applause around the table and lots of smiles. Dr. Qxilo nodded as he mouthed, "Thank you."

That evening, after supper, Yung spoke up, "I would like to acknowledge the elephant that is in the room."

Julie exclaimed, "The what?"

Mack interjected, "It's an idiom for, 'there is a problem that we may be reticent to talk about.'"

Julie shrugged, "Oh."

Yung continued, "Since we have lost Ibram, we are left with a two male and three female crew." They all looked questioningly at one another. She continued, "Mike and Mack are married, but that leaves Dr. Qxilo with the two of us."

Akilah spoke up, "I would just like to state, for the record, that I am perfectly content being single."

To this Yung replied, "And you just expect me to…" and left the sentence unfinished.

Akilah smiled. "That is between the two of you. I just wanted to take myself out of the biological running," and her smile broadened.

Dr. Qxilo was now smiling too. He reached over and placed his hand on top of Yung's. "We will talk later."

She pulled her hand away. "You bet we will!" she stated emphatically! "This is not a forgone conclusion!"

Julie added, "And you won't be lonely, Akilah. You'll still have me," and she too smiled.

Akilah stated, "Good! It's settled then."

Yung quipped, "It most certainly is not!" By now everyone else was smiling. "Humph!" she exclaimed as she got up and left the table.

Still smiling, Julie stated the obvious, "So, that's what an elephant looks like?" The rest of them laughed lightly.

Dr. Qxilo looked after Yung and said, "Neurosis?"

They continued to laugh, all except Julie, who said, "Huh?"

Still smiling, Dr. Qxilo explained, "Psychiatrist joke."

Yung kept mostly to herself the entire next week. She spent most of her time in one of the gardens or another. She ate at different times than the rest of the team, even after Akilah had approached her and apologized if she had offended her. Still, she kept to herself. It was finally Julie who broke the ice.

She had been keeping track of her, she did have access to all of the ship's cameras, and had found her in one of the gardens. "Is there anything I can do to help?"

Yung said nonchalantly, "Grab a pair of pruners." She held hers out to Julie in demonstration. " Here is how you use them." Julie grabbed a pair. They walked up to a fruit tree. "See this new growth? They are called suckers and need to be removed. Next, when you have branches that are crossed, you remove the smaller, younger branch. Finally, when you have a number of branches coming out a single branch, remove all but one of them." Soon the ground was littered in branches. When they were done with a single tree, they cut all the fallen branches into lengths of about the span of a hand. This would aid in their decomposition. They gathered them into a bucket and moved to the next tree.

They worked in silence, side by side, for the next hour. Then Yung sat down in the grass. "Thank you for not forcing me to talk about anything." Julie just nodded. Yung continued, "I don't like to be forced to do things. I know that wasn't Akilah's intention, but it just didn't seem to leave any room for options. I guess that is what offended me. It precluded that Dr. Qxilo and I would get together and didn't seem to leave me with any choice to the contrary."

"You could always seduce Mike," Julie spoke up.

"That's horrid, and betray Mack?" Yung exclaimed.

Julie was smiling a little, "True, but a choice nonetheless."

Yung saw Julie's smile and realized it was an attempt at a joke. She smiled in return. "That is still a silly idea," she stated.

Julie's smile broadened, "I know. Human conversation is not necessarily my strong suite."

Yung laughed lightly, "And yet, you are pretty adept at it."

Julie bowed her head, "Thank you." She said looking at the dirt.

Yung joined them for lunch and announced, "I'm sorry. I have been acting so standoffish."

To which Julie responded, "What kind of fish?"

Yung continued, "Keeping away from you all, being all by myself."

Julie still looked confused, "I still don't see what that has to do with fish? Oh, like the elephant?" Then she laughed.

And they all laughed.

It was Mike who broached the subject. "Ibram has been frozen since his death. What if we harvested his sperm and kept it in case we needed it?"

Dr. Qxilo spoke up, "It might solve the genetic narrowing problem the colony will experience without him."

Julie looked around, "What do the rest of you think?" There was a general nodding of heads. "Okay, I will do it some evening after you have all gone to sleep." They left the harvesting up to her.

Chapter Twenty-Two
Into Orbit

Their observation of Mars had visually expanded daily until the planet encompassed all they could see on that side of the ship. Julie passed out a seven-inch by nine-inch hand-held electronic tablet to each of them. "We have entered into our Martian orbit, as you can tell by," and she pointed out the window. "These contain the checklists of the items that must be visually and/or manually verified as ready in preparation for landing. I estimate that it will take us two days to complete the checklists. In the meantime, I will continue to monitor all of the ship's systems. Off you go." She sounded like a mother hen releasing her chicks.

Regardless, four of them were each off to one of the gardens. Mack began her checklist of items in the main part of the ship.

When they met for dinner that evening, true to plan, they were each about halfway through their checklists. The wall of the dining area that contained the food processing unit was now a single panel capable of showing a projection. They had finished supper and now faced the panel.

Julie addressed them, pointing to the projected image on the panel. "This is the site chosen for our landing and the initial settlement of our Martian colony as of a few months ago. As you recall, preceding our departure, a robotic excavation team was sent to the planet. It was their duty to prepare the site for our arrival." The image changed. "Here is the site as of yesterday."

What had been a rocky plain as far as the eye could see, was now a sculptured flat field of smooth reddish brown dirt.

Mars has been prepared to receive its first human colony.

They all sat on the edge of their seats, entranced with the view of their landing site.

The next day they all finished their checklists without a hitch. At supper they shared their similarly successful completions.

Mack spoke up for them all, "So, Julie, we're ready?"

Julie smiled warmly. "We'll begin our descent to Mars right after breakfast in the morning."

Dr. Qxilo went off to bed. Julie went forward to the control room. The rest of them went to the Great Room, lay on the floor, and watched Mars move across the sky above them until it filled their vision.

Breakfast was uneventful.

Julie asked them to return to their hibernation pods. "They are supposed to be the safest place in the ship and while I do not foresee any problems with the landing, it probably pays to be extra cautious since this is the first landing of a Ying-Yang propulsion driven ship carrying four garden pods onto another planet. It will take most of the day, as our descent will be slow. You may want to bring something into the pod with you so you won't be bored. Mack will stay with me in the control area just in case I need her expertise."

Mike chose to listen to classical music. Dr. Qxilo took his electronic pad with him in order to review some recent medical journals. Yung was in the middle of a book on her pad, while Akilah was reading up on the latest search for water on Mars. Their descent went smoothly and many hours later they finally reached the surface of the planet.

There was no jolt, just Julie's announcement, "We have landed."

Almost in unison the four of them touched the hibernation pod controls, which opened to allow them to swing their legs over and to stand up.

Mike asked, "Shall we grab our helmets and gloves and go out and check out the planet Mars?"

Julie responded with a simple, "Yes."

The suits reconfigured their nano-bytes to become air-tight. They put on their soft helmets and gloves. They helped one another to slip into their re-breathing backpacks and connected them to their suits. They added individual front packs of tools and special implements and were ready to brave all things Martian: the atmosphere, the terrain, and anything else they might discover.

Part Two
Welcome to Aries

Chapter Twenty-Three
Introduction to Mars

They stood in the airlock, Yung, with Julie behind her, the other four in front of them. They were making a record of the first Martian colonists stepping out onto the Martian landscape. It was an historic moment. Yung took photos and Julie captured video footage through a device that utilized her left eye as its video lens. A stairway of three steps descended to the Martian floor. They stepped out onto the top stair and turned around.

Mack spoke for them all. "We are about to make history. We have been unable to prove that there has ever been life on Mars, but today that all changes. Today begins the establishment of the first colony of life on Mars from Earth. A new chapter in the history of both planets." She turned and held out her hands to the others. All four of them joined hands, stepped down the stairs together, and onto the ground of Mars. Yung then handed her camera to Julie and walked down the steps herself.

Julie addressed them all, "You need to take a stroll around the garden pods and the ship and confirm that everything is okay. I'll see you back in the dining hall for supper."

Mike and Mack saluted her, the others just waved and went to their separate garden pods. Mack spent her time inspecting the ship's fuselage and the solar panels that now lay outstretched on the Martian floor. Mike finished his garden pod quickly and then found Mack and aided her in the inspection of the solar panels. When they were through, they concluded that everything seemed to have landed without any damage.

At supper, all the reports were the same. Everything seemed to indicate that the first descent of a Ying-Yang powered ship onto another planet had gone off without a hitch. After supper they all went about their own personal duties.

Akilah went outside the ship, which they now called the compound since it had permanently landed. The Martian sunset was nothing compared to that on earth, the sun being so far away, but it did still occur almost every twenty-four hours, plus about forty minutes, a soft glow slowly receding behind her. The light and the stillness displayed their own brand of beauty. She walked to the edge of the compound and stood next to the vehicle building. Some movement caught her eye. She stepped around the building.

There it stood.

It was about two and a half meters tall and would have appeared gangly on earth for its thinness. It appeared to be fully clothed in a tightly scaled reddish tan armor, with something in its hand. Was it a walking stick, perhaps, maybe a weapon? A trickle of fear dribbled slowly down her back and her heart began to pound.

The words formed clearly in her mind, "You need not be afraid, I mean you no harm. I thought it time that we met."

The fear did begin to fade. Then the being pointed the staff in her direction and the tip began to glow a deep red in the light evening's setting sun. Was there a light on its end? A gem maybe? Suddenly it glinted, as though the sun had struck it directly. The being was gone. Now Akilah was unsure if she had really seen it or just imagined the entire encounter.

She sank shakily to her knees. Then she heard something behind her. She struggled to stand, but did so and turned to find Julie standing there.

Julie whispered, "What? What have you seen?"

The words stumbled out of Akilah, "I'm not sure."

Julie went on, "Was he carrying a staff tipped with a red gem?"

Akilah's eyes widened as she thought, *"How could Julie possibly know that?"* She nodded.

Julie slowly fell to her own knees, folded her hands, and bowed her head as she proclaimed, "It is him, Odemel. This is his planet. Tell no one what you have just seen. Tomorrow evening, he will take you on an adventure that will be difficult to explain to the others, but you can trust him."

Wide-eyed, Akilah simply nodded her assent.

That next evening after supper, Akilah announced, "I'm going to take a little walk before I turn in."

Julie added, "I'll go out with you."

They were about fifty meters out when Odemel suddenly appeared out of nowhere. He still did not need to speak out loud, "Take my hand," and he extended it towards Akilah.

She took a slow deep breath, "Julie says I can trust you."

He smiled. It was comforting, "You can."

She had a question, "Why do I hear your words in my head, but we must speak them with our mouths when we speak to each other?"

"Ah, First Speech. It is a spiritual language, spoken before the Fall. We still speak it here. After the Fall, Adam spoke with his mouth, 'I hid because I was naked.' That was second speech, but still universal until the Tower of Babel, when speech was confused into languages."

Akilah inquired somewhat sheepishly, "Can you read my mind?"

Odemel smiled, "Yes and it is a mess," he laughed. "Sorry, my feeble attempt at humor. No, I cannot read your mind, only what is directed to me. Does that help?"

She nodded and took his hand. They walked further into the Martian plain.

He stopped, opened his arms and whispered, "Come into my embrace."

Akilah looked questioningly at Julie, who nodded. She stepped close to him and he wrapped his arms around her, careful not to hit her with his staff. She realized that he was not wearing armor, but that his skin was tightly scaled like that of a beautiful snake. He looked to Julie and winked. There was a rumble and they were gone.

Julie stood there looking at the plain. It showed no evidence that it had just swallowed them up, but they were gone. She sighed, turned, walked back to the compound, and entered the airlock.

The rest of the crew were discussing tomorrow's projects when Julie walked in alone and stood there. She whispered, "Something strange has happened. Akilah is gone."

Mike bolted to his feet, "What happened?"

She looked at the floor, "About seventy-five meters into the plain, she just disappeared. You may have felt the rumble. I must I have been looking away, but when I looked back she was gone. I went to where she had been standing. There was nothing. It was though she had simply vanished."

Mike ran to the airlock, followed closely by Mack, both grabbing their helmets, gloves, and rebreathing packs along the way. They helped each other gear up and entered the lock with Julie, who of course needed no helmet or rebreathing apparatus.

Outside, Mike exclaimed, "Where?" Julie pointed and he sprinted the seventy-five yards and then began examining the ground. Just as Julie had said, there was no evidence of any disturbance. He pointed to the ground, "Here?"

Julie nodded.

"But there is nothing. Both your footprints just stop and then yours turn around and go back to the ship."

Mack had followed, but at a walk, looking left, right, up and down all the way. She confirmed his observations. There was nothing, no evidence as to what had happened to Akilah.

"What are we to do?" Mack exclaimed, excitedly.

Julie took a deep breath, "I don't know what to do. It is an enigma."

The rest of the crew joined them. They milled around for a bit and then returned to the ship.

They all sat around the table. Dr. Qxilo spoke, "You said there was a rumble? We felt something, a slight vibration. Then what happened?"

Julie looked down at the table again, then back up, "When I looked around to where she had been, she was no longer there."

Now it was Yung's turn, "And what was the rumble?"

Julie held her gaze, "I have no idea."

Yung began to weep. Dr. Qxilo put his arm around her and she shrugged it off. They all just sat there.

Chapter Twenty-Four
His Home

A kilah had closed her eyes. When she opened them, she was still in Odemel's embrace, but they stood in a room somewhere. The lighting was subdued, but you could see just fine. He opened his arms and she stepped out of his embrace. There was a low table there and some cushions. The table appeared laden with plates of some kind of fruit and container of some kind of drink. Odemel pointed to the table, "Will you join me? Oh, you can remove your helmet here, the atmosphere is compatible with human life."

She removed her helmet, gloves, and tucked them into her belt.

He held out his hand palm upward, "I am Odemel."

She placed her hand in his and he brought it to his lips to lightly kiss it as she said, "Akilah."

She reclined and he poured her some of the drink. "You are familiar with the term 'Malak' from the Quran?"

"Yes," she said softly, "it means 'angel.' He bowed his head towards her slightly, pointing his fingers to his chest. "You are an angel?" He nodded. "Julie said this was your planet."

He smiled. Although not a human, he was basically humanoid. While thin, he did have two arms, two legs, a torso, neck, head, and was covered in a tightly scaled skin of reddish tan. His smile was comforting. "Not my planet as in ownership, but as in governance." He, too, reclined, "My angels and I have been orchestrating life on this planet for a long time."

There were knives of an alien metal next to fired clay plates. He picked his up, stabbed a fruit and placed it on his plate. He motioned for her to do the same as he handed her a clay goblet he had filled for her. He folded his hands, which only had a thumb and three fingers. He neither bowed his head nor closed his eyes, but just spoke as though someone else were sitting there. "Thank you for providing all we need and so much more, and for safely bringing Akilah and her companions here." He paused and his eyes might have moistened. "I'm sorry, I believe that you lost one of them to an asteroid."

She scowled, *"How on earth could he know that,"* she, too, paused, *"unless he truly was an angel."* She finally stammered, "Yes, Ibram, my countryman," and she looked at the table.

His words were as comforting as his tone had been. "But you would say that he is now with God, would you not?"

She looked up.

"You may grieve his loss, but not the state of his soul."

She looked away, sighed, and slowly nodded, "**Yes**."

He raised his cup, "To the future, as uncertain as it may seem at the moment."

She smiled weakly, "To the future."

They each sipped their drink. Akilah found it lightly fruity and vaguely sweet without being over-bearing.

Odemel set his goblet down, picked up his knife and sliced a piece off the fruit.

"You may consume its skin as well," and he took a bite. "As I am sure you know, angels do not need to eat, drink, or sleep, but we are able to do so. It makes us seem more like you or like the Ma-adeem who live here."

She sliced a piece and also took a bite. It was similar to the drink although more pungent in both aroma and taste. She smiled slightly, "Hmm, it is good."

"Yes, you will find our planet is untainted by the darkness that envelopes yours. Is there provision for us in the Quran?" he asked.

She thought a moment, "I believe so, but the verse escapes me."

He continued for her, "In Surah Al-Shurah it states, 'The creation of the heavens and the earth and living things He has spread forth in both and they are some of His signs.' which would imply living things throughout the heavens. That might only refer to the Malak or it might include other beings on other planets. Yours, however, is the only planet that rebelled and is therefore labeled as 'dark' or under the influence of the 'dark one.' The Hebrews would say that it lies 'under the power of the evil one.' What do you know of Jesus?"

She squinted, wondering where this was going, "He is a prophet."

"Yet in Surah Ali Imran it calls him 'the Messiah.' No other prophet is called 'the messiah.' What does 'messiah' mean?"

Still wondering, she replied, "I believe it means anointed for a specific purpose?"

"And Jesus' purpose?"

She shrugged.

"A little later it states that he will restore the blind, cleanse the leper, and raise the dead. What other prophets raised the dead?"

Again she thought a moment, then responded, "Elijah raised the widow at Zarapheth's son."

He smiled his infectious smile again, "Correct, but Jesus raised Jarius' daughter whom had just died; the widow's son when she was on her way to Nain to bury him; and Lazarus, who had been dead so long they were afraid there would be a stink. That seems like more than just a prophet. Jesus seems special."

She had to agree.

Odemel then asked Akilah, "May I tell you a story?"

She cut another slice of fruit, "Sure."

He began, "One day Jesus was in a home teaching. The home was so full of people that there was nowhere to sit or even stand any longer. There was even a crowd of people outside listening to him through the open door and windows. There was also a paralytic with four friends who wanted to bring him to Jesus, but there was no way that they could get close. So, they carried him up to the open roof, made the opening larger, and then lowered the paralytic down to just in front of Jesus. When Jesus saw their faith, He said to the paralytic, 'Son, your sins are forgiven.' The religious leaders who were there were incensed, 'Who does this man think that he is. This is blasphemy! Only God can forgive sin.' Meanwhile, Jesus, perceiving in His spirit their questioning, said, 'Why do you question these things in your hearts? Which is easier, to say to the paralytic, 'Your sins are forgiven,' or to say, 'Rise, take up your bed and walk'? But that you may know that the Son of Man has authority on earth to forgive sins, He paused and turned to the paralytic, 'I say to you, rise, pick up your bed, and go home.' And the paralyzed man rose and immediately picked up his bed and went out before them all, so that they were all amazed and glorified God, saying, 'We never saw anything like this!'"

Odemel looked deeply into Akilah's eyes and asked, "Would you like Him to do that for you, forgive your sins?"

She scowled, "I thought it was just a story?"

He smiled, "A true one nonetheless."

Her face softened, "He can do that?"

Odemel sighed, "I know your Quran implies that his crucifixion was a mistake, but it wasn't fake or a mistake. Regarding His exaltation, His ascension, it is correct. He died to pay the penalty for your sins and rose from the dead to reconnect you to God. Again, would you like Him to do that for you?"

A tear formed in her eye, as she simply said, "Yes."

Odemel continued, "Just ask Him to do so, out loud, like He was sitting right there," and he pointed to an empty cushion.

She looked to the empty cushion, and began, "Jesus, please forgive my sins," and she hesitated.

Odemel prompted her, "and reconnect me to God."

She followed his lead, "And please, reconnect me to God."

"Now close your eyes and take a slow deep breath."

She did.

"Another one."

She did that too.

"One more."

She took one final deep breath. Tears were now streaming down her face.

"You feel that?" he asked.

She nodded slightly.

"That's Him. You will never be alone again."

Chapter Twenty-Five
Meanwhile at the Compound

They looked around the compound for days and still had found nothing, not a trace of Akilah anywhere and no sign of what had happened to her. Julie knew the answer to both of those questions, but she was not supposed to tell them.

Dr. Qxilo spoke up, Perhaps we should take a short break in our search and bury Ibram." He pointed to the small hill behind the compound. "Mike and I could go up there and prepare a place for his body."

Mike agreed, "Yeah," and paused, that a might be a good idea."

The rest of them looked at the ground and shrugged their shoulders.

"I'll be right back." He went in and came back out with two shovels.

He and Dr. Qxilo went up the hill and spent the next hour digging a hole in which to place the body. When they felt they had an adequate hole, they came back, put his body on a stretcher in a large bag, and all accompanied them up to the top of the hill. Mike and Dr. Qxilo lowered Ibram into the grave.

Julie spoke first, "Any last words?"

Yung took a deep breath, "If Akilah were here she would say a Dua for him. Something like, 'Forgive Ibram and bring him to a place alongside those You are guiding. Shed light along his path as he continues his journey with You, O Master of the Universe. Have mercy on us all and reunite us when the time is right.'" She reached down for a handful of dirt and let it fall into the grave on top of the body bag in which they had placed him when they had retrieved him from his hibernation pod.

Dr. Qxilo added, "He had so wanted to be here. It was his life's ambition." He sighed, "Well, he is here, not as the first man to set foot on Mars, but the first to personally discover its depths, " he smiled weakly, "maybe even some of its secrets." He added his handful of dirt.

Mike reached over and took Mack's hand, then directed his words towards the hole, "We will do our best to make you proud of what we will establish here." They both reached down, picked up a handful of dirt and dropped it in on top of the bag.

Dr. Qxilo and Mike picked up their shovels and began filling the hole as the ladies stood by, tears in their eyes. As an android, Julie didn't weep. She did understand grief and loss, but knew that Ibram wasn't really dead. He just was not there with them. They finished filling the hole and the five of them turned to retrace their steps down the hill.

There stood Akilah.

She smiled, "Take me to your leader," she smiled weakly.

Mike exclaimed, "Where have you been?"

Dr. Qxilo demanded, "How are you alive?"

Mack cried out at the same time, "We have been so worried."

Yung ran to her and hugged her.

Her smiled softened as she stepped out of Yung's embrace, "You'll need to be sitting down," and she turned back towards the ship.

They followed her, confused, bewildered, but relieved that she had suddenly and seemingly miraculously returned.

Chapter Twenty-Six
The Explanation

Dr. Qxilo tried to take command of the situation, "Before we do anything, I want to check you out in the Infirmary."

Akilah stopped and turned to face him, "No, I am fine. You'll understand after I have explained what happened."

Dr. Qxilo insisted, "You can explain all you want, but first you're going to the infirmary."

Akilah took a step closer and looked him straight in the eye, "No, there is no need."

Dr. Qxilo placed his hands on his hips, "I must insist, for the health and safety of us all. You have been gone for days, on an alien planet. You must be checked out."

Akilah looked at Julie and pleaded, "Julie?"

Julie spoke in slow and measured words, "Doctor, I know you mean well, but if Akilah says she is fine, we must trust her. Let's hear what she has to say first."

"Humph!" Dr. Qxilo huffed. "I don't know how she might be infected, but I'm putting on my helmet and gloves," and he stomped off.

Finally, when they all sat around the dining room table, they fixed their eyes on Akilah,

"I know that you have a million questions and I hope to have anticipated most of them, but first, Julie, do we have anything stronger than tea to drink?"

"You mean something alcoholic, like wine?" Julie surmised.

Akilah sighed contentedly, "Yes, that would be wonderful."

Dr. Qxilo pointed to his helmet, "None for me."

Akilah just shook her head, rolling her eyes.

Julie returned with the wine she had produced seemingly out of thin air and began filling cups and passing them about.

Akilah lifted her cup and they all followed suit, "To understanding."

Dr. Qxilo had nothing to toast with.

The others repeated, "To understanding," and each took a small sip.

Mike chortled, "Wow, that's quite good."

Julie's smiled.

Akilah began, "First, Mars is inhabited,"

There was a sharp intake of breath by them all.

"And I was approached and transported by one of the inhabitants. There was no sinister intent, I assure you. He simply wanted to introduce himself to me and needed some time to bring me up to speed. You are familiar with the concept of angels?"

There was a general nodding of heads.

"In the Judeo-Christian and Muslim traditions, they were created before man to rule the universe. Man was created to rule the planet Earth, a task which he hasn't done very well. One of the archangel's commanders was given Mars to rule and asked to lead the native Martians here. It was he who stood before me. He is about two and a half meters tall and basically humanoid. He has a head, arms and legs, and he is rather slim. He spoke to me in what I would assume is a telepathic language that I could understand without translation. I do not believe that he could read my mind, but I do know that I didn't need to speak out loud in order for him to understand me."

She paused for a drink, "He has been ruling here since the dawn of time and, because Martians did not participate in the rebellion, ruling in peace and harmony. However, there is some concern that we might contaminate this world with the darkness and corruption that is on Earth. To help mitigate against that possibility, he introduced me to Jesus."

Dr. Qxilo spoke up, "He what?"

Akilah smiled almost shyly, "He introduced me to Jesus. He did so rather compassionately from the Quran."

Mike's was astonished, "Jesus is in the Quran?"

"Most definitely, and while we revere him as a prophet, he showed me that Jesus is much more than a prophet, and still alive and present today. Then, he introduced me to him."

Mack jumped in, "This is all a bit overwhelming. Mars is inhabited with angels, and they know Jesus?"

Akilah looked at her, her eyes moist with emotion, "Of course, they have met him. These are real angels I am talking about, and a real Jesus." She looked at Mike and then back to Mack, "You both, I believe, were raised in the Christian tradition. So you know Jesus, or at least about him. However," and she paused, "have you met Him?"

They both looked sheepishly at each other and then shook their heads, *"No."*

She looked at Yung and Dr. Qxilo, "And what is the Chinese tradition concerning Jesus?"

Yung looked down at the table. "From ancient times we have heard about the Dao, often translated as the Path or the Way. The missionaries told us that Jesus claimed to be 'the Way.'"

Akilah smiled at them, "Yes, and 'the Truth,' and 'the Life.' He desires that you not only know the Way, but that you be personally connected to it, to him. Would you like that, to be connected to him?" They all looked at one another as she continued, "It's really a pretty simple two-step process. You ask him to forgive your sins. Those are the things that you have done that have separated you from God and that Jesus died in order to take away. Then, secondly, you ask him to reconnect you to God and he will. Just speak to him, out loud, like he was sitting next to Julie. He is here, after all, you just can't see him."

Mike reached out and took Mack's hand, "Jesus, please forgive my sins," and he paused while Mack added, "And mine, too." He took a deep breath and continued, "and reconnect us to God." They waited, still holding hands. Then both their eyes widened and they looked at each other, as tears filled their eyes.

Mack whispered, "I think he just did."

Akilah nodded and looked to Dr. Qxilo and Yung.

He gestured towards Yung, "Ladies first."

She gulped, "Jesus, I, too, would like my sins removed and to be reconnected to God."

Dr. Qxilo watched her closely as tears filled her eyes. She smiled through her tears and nodded towards him.

He shook his head, "It really can't be that easy."

Akilah responded, "Yes, it can."

He frowned, "You know, you can't force me to do this."

At the other end of the ship they heard the "whoosh" that sounded like the airlock opening. They all looked that direction, and in walked a slim, tall, humanoid-looking being, covered in what appeared to be a tightly scaled armor, and holding a staff topped with a red jewel.

The words formed authoritatively in their minds, "I am Odemel. This is my planet. You have come here of your own free will, but it is up to me whether you may stay here."

Dr. Qxilo looked at the others, who slid out of their chairs to take a knee before Odemel as though he were royalty.

Dr. Qxilo stood defiantly, "And you would have me believe that you are an angel?" He paused as Odemel nodded, then said sarcastically, "Well, then, do something angelic!"

Odemel lifted his staff a few centimeters off the floor and brought it back down with a resounding clank as light burst from the jewel. "He was made a little lower than the angels, then he died for you. However, he did not stay dead, he rose from the dead and can reconnect you to God, as some of you can now testify." Odemel paused and looked towards Mike, "When Moses asked God for a sign that would prove to the people that he was sent from God, what did Moses do?"

Mike thought a moment, and then replied, "Threw down his staff on the ground as God had asked him to and it became a snake."

Odemel took the gem off of the top of his staff, put it into a fold in his robe, and dropped the staff to the ground. It became a snake. They all instantly recoiled from it. It slithered towards Dr. Qxilo. He was petrified with fear.

Odemel said, "Doctor, reach down and pick up the snake by his tail."

Dr. Qxilo looked at Odemel with obvious fear in his eyes.

Odemel continued, "You asked me…" and he left the sentence trailing.

Slowly, Dr. Qxilo bent over as the snake circled around him, and picked it up by the tail. It turned back into a staff. Odemel reached out a hand for the staff and the doctor gave it to him.

Odemel continued, "When you drag a finger down the front of your suit, the nano-bytes in the material unzip it. Do that."

Dr. Qxilo did so, and his suit unzipped.

"Now, with your left hand, open the flap of your suit and place your right hand inside the flap." He did that too. "Now, remove your hand."

When Dr. Qxilo removed his hand from his suit, it was white with leprosy. He stepped back, startled, and almost stumbled. Odemel spoke again, "The second sign. Now, place your hand back in the suit."

He did so, shakily.

"Remove it once again."

When he removed his hand the second time it was restored to normal.

"Is that good enough for you, or do you need some more evidence?"

Dr. Qxilo looked at the front, then the back, of his hand, "No, no, no, that is enough. I believe that you are truly an angel." He paused, "Which means that the rest of what you said is also true?"

Odemel nodded.

"And while I consider myself a rather exemplary human being, the good things that I have not done and the wrong things that I have done still separate me from God?"

Odemel nodded again.

Dr. Qxilo actually knelt, and continued, "but Jesus died to take away those things." He looked at the ground, "So…... Jesus, please take away my wrong." His voice broke, "and please reconnect me to God." He brought his head down to the floor and began to weep. He wept for a few minutes. Then stopping, he lifted his head, smiled weakly, and clutching his chest, said, as he looked at Odemel, "Is that what he feels like?"

Odemel nodded a final time. "Now, you are all reconnected."

Mike spoke up, "What about Julie?"

Odemel smiled, "Ah, she was created connected and has never done wrong. Tomorrow, I will show you what we have been working on for you. Have a wonderful evening." In the blink of an eye, he was gone.

They all looked at Akilah as Mike spoke again, "Now, that was interesting."

Chapter Twenty-Seven
The City

The next morning at breakfast, Julie announced that they were all requested to join Odemel outside and travel to his city.

They stood before him as he spoke, "The entrance to my city and all of underground Mars is protected. You can only enter or exit it in the presence of me or one of my angels. Please form a circle and hold hands with one another."

They did so.

Odemel placed one hand on Akilah's shoulder and lifted his staff to hold in the other hand, a few centimeters off the ground. He muttered something as he brought its end back down to the planet's surface, and amidst a flash of light and a percussion of wind, they were translated from where they had stood to a plaza in Odemel's city. To call it a city might be an overstatement. It was more like a rudimentary town square. One side was completely taken up by small stalls of food. There were a few people putting out their produce in the stalls, but the square itself was mostly vacant. The people were smaller versions of Odemel, a little less than two meters tall, with the same reddish tan scaled skin, thin, and gangly.

On the other side of the market there was a small stone temple and beyond it a small stone, almost palace-like home. It was much more endearing than ostentatious. Odemel strode off in the direction of the home. There were no guards, probably because on Mars they were unnecessary. They walked through a courtyard and entered a large open doorway to find a stone entry and two angels about ten centimeters shorter than Odemel.

One held a large bowl of liquid. The other held a large hand towel. As the crew and Odemel entered, the other two knelt, the one placing the bowl on the ground. Odemel set his staff against a table that was just inside the doorway.

"You will find the atmosphere here breathable. You may remove your rebreather packs, helmets, gloves, and boots." He pointed to the kneeling pair. "These are two of my angels. You will notice that they are somewhat taller than the natives who were in the square, but shorter than I. They will wash your feet, a custom we have here."

Mike spoke up, "Is that water? It looks like water."

Odemel smiled, "Yes, there is water on Mahdeem. Your name for this planet is Mars, ours is Mahdeem. One of our gifts to you will be access to enough water for your colony to survive. That we use water to wash your feet makes the ceremony that much more special." The two angels washed and dried Odemel's feet.

Odemel motioned Dr. Qxilo forward. The first angel reached out to receive his right foot, placed it in the water and nearly sang, "Welcome to our home." The other angel dried his foot with a, "May your stay with us be especially blessed." Dr. Qxilo had tears in his eyes as they dried his left foot. Odemel motioned for the doctor to enter the next room. Yung stepped forward to have her feet washed, as did Mike, Mack, and Akilah. In the next room was a low table surrounded by cushions. It seemed there must be trees on the planet somewhere. They each stood by one of the cushions until Odemel moved to the head of the table. There was a place setting at each cushion location with a clay plate, metal knife, small cloth and clay goblet. At the foot of the table there was an empty cushion complete with its own place setting.

Odemel spoke as though addressing the unoccupied cushion, "You provide all that we need and for that we are thankful. May our time together be productive and blessed." He added, "You may be seated."

They all reclined at the table.

"Again, welcome to my planet. I don't own it, I am just in charge of maintaining and orchestrating its governance, which is not very difficult as nothing evil exists here. That is why we are so concerned that you might bring your evil to our planet."

Dr. Qxilo spoke up, "Do you think that introducing us to Jesus will solve the problem?"

Odemel took a slow deep breath before speaking, "It should surely help, if you will listen to him." Then he smiled and lifted a goblet, "To an evil-less friendship between our two planets,"

Dr. Qxilo went on, "Well, we can't speak for the entire planet of Earth, but it is not our intent to bring evil here, and it never has been."

Odemel's smile dimmed, "Regardless of your intent, evil tends to accompany your race. It is like a contagion. You bring it with you wherever you go." He sighed. After a pause when no one spoke, he invited, "Please, try the fruit." They sat for a moment, just eating silently, then Odemel asked, "Would you like to see my town," and he smiled, "and the fields that surround it?"

Mack answered before the others, "Am I to assume that we are underground?"

Odemel's smile grew, "You are correct."

Mack squinted, "Where does the light come from?"

"Ah...." Odemel lengthened the word, "a good question." He paused, "When God said, 'Let there be light,' he didn't just make light of one kind, like sunlight, but many kinds of light. One of those kinds exists here, underground, capable of growing our crops."

Mack went on to say, "So, it's light here all the time, always light, with no dark?"

Odemel smiled, "It could be like that, but he decided that half a day of light and half a day without would allow us to mark time. We also have calendars, but do not mark time by the hour. You can say 'Meet me about mid-day.' We do not need to be very accurate about time because we have lots of it." He looked at Dr. Qxilo. "Because there is no evil here, there is no sickness nor death, either accidental or otherwise, and no need for 'hurry.'"

The doctor screwed up his face, "How old are you?"

Odemel's smile continued, "We are all about the same age. It took a few years to get to an optimal number across the planet and we have just stayed at that number."

Yung was shocked, "No children?"

Odemel lifted his shoulders, "Not required. You may not have noticed, the people are male and female. The males are about two centimeters taller and the females more broad at the hip."

Yung shook her head, "But children are such a blessing..." and she left the sentence open.

Odemel sighed, "Life here is such a blessing, all of it, everyday. You probably wonder if it gets boring? The same old wonderful life, free of sickness and pain, no heartache or trouble. I can assure you, his vastness is unsearchable.

There is no end to his wonder. I once jokingly asked him if he would like to send the people of Earth here as a preview of heaven. He said that he might consider it. Maybe you are his test case." He smiled again. He looked them over, "Well, should we go take a look?"

They nodded.

As they headed for the door, he added, "One of my angels will escort each of you at all times, so I will pair you up with one now."

Odemel stood outside the door as Dr. Qxilo exited the house. Five of the angels stood there waiting. They were simply a smaller version of Odemel, a little over two meters tall. They all looked pretty similar. It would take some time to be able to tell them apart.

Dr. Qxilo was thinking, *"Name tags would have been nice."*

Odemel began, "This is Sheen," and Sheen nodded and began to walk alongside Dr. Qxilo.

Yung was next, "This is Nefesh."

Next came Akilah, "This is Cinam."

Mike and Mack walked out together, "Mike, this is Keli, and Mack, this is Labub."

Mack looked back as Julie stepped out of the house, "What about Julie?"

Odemel laughed lightly, "She will be stuck with me. You may ask your guardians anything you like as we walk through the town and towards our fields."

Chapter Twenty-Eight
A Walkabout

They walked to the market which contained no shops. Items were simply displayed in open stalls. It appeared that their culture was not competitive. The market selection process was orderly. The people looked like scaled down angels. There was no yelling or arguing, simply people making selections, but nothing changed hands so it appeared to be cashless. Each vendor provided a single kind of item, and had a tablet that the purchaser marked before he selected his item and signed with some kind of stylus. He then went over and selected the quantity that he had signed for. There were a few angels around, but no obvious policing of the area.

Dr. Qxilo asked Sheen, "How are people making purchases? I don't see any money changing hands?"

Sheen shrugged, looked at Odemel, then answered, "I am unfamiliar with the word 'money'. If you wish to purchase an item, you grant the vendor so many Ashrah towards a product or service that you can later provide to that vendor. For instance, say I am a vendor of Taenah. I have been purchasing Anavaheem from you for a month and you have accumulated one hundred of my Ashrah. You might use those Ashrah with me and have me give you some of my Taenah for some of your Ashrah. Does that make sense?"

Dr. Qxilo answered, "Yes, I think I understand, but I saw no bartering either."

Sheen again looked at him quizzically, "Bartering?"

Dr. Qxilo went on, "If, say, I feel this Anavaheem is worth two Ashrah, but you want three for it. How do we come to agreement?"

Sheen appeared more befuddled. "It's my produce. Why would you want it for less than I say it is worth?"

Dr. Qxilo looked sideways. "Hmm, I guess there is no bartering."

Sheen shook his head, "'Bartering, what a funny concept."

"Incidentally," Dr. Qxilo replied, "What is an Anavaheem?"

Sheen took him over to a stall of what looked like a variety of fruits and pointed to a very large blackberry, half the size of his fist.

"How much is it?" Dr. Qxilo inquired.

Sheen smiled, "Three Ashrah."

Dr. Qxilo shook his head. "What if I wanted one? I have no Ashrah."

Sheen looked away for a moment, then back, "I could purchase it for you and you could owe me three Ashrah."

Dr. Qxilo wrinkled up his nose, "You would do that?"

Sheen wrinkled up his own nose, "I will assume that you have some product or service I would like in the future."

Dr. Qxilo still pondered, "You would loan me three Ashrah on that assumption?"

"Loan?" and he cocked his head to the right. "It is a covenant promise between us."

Dr. Qxilo looked back at the others, "Ok, I'll have one."

Yung piped up, "I think you forgot the magic word."

Dr. Qxilo glowered at her like a petulant child, "Please, may I have an Anavaheem?"

Sheen signed the tablet, picked out a good one, a small cloth, and handed it to Dr. Qxilo. "Consider it a gift."

Dr. Qxilo took it thinking, *"Hmmm, that's an even greater indebtedness than giving him my promise."* He took a bite. It was very good, extremely juicy, and he was very glad he had been provided a cloth. He wondered what material the cloth was made of. Wonderingly he asked, "From what material is this cloth?"

Sheen grinned as though proud, "It is woven from plant fibers."

Mike pointed to what looked like a purple apple and asked Keli, "What are those?"

He responded, "They are Inveem. Would you like one?"

Mike was afraid to ask, but did so anyway, "How much are they?"

Keli smiled, "They are also only three Ashrah?"

Mike wrinkled his brow, "Why did you say 'only' three Ashrah?"

His smile nearly split his face in two, "Because I like them even more than the Anavaheem. Would you like one?"

Mike looked to Yung as he replied, "Yes, please." Keli purchased one, signed on the shopkeeper's tablet, and handed it to him as he took out his own little tablet and had him sign for it.

"Thank you." He bit into it. It was more like a large grape and he was glad for a cloth, too. It seemed the perfect balance between sweetness and tartness. Although he had not tasted Dr. Qxilo's Anavaheem, he was very pleased with his selection.

Mack had stopped two stalls further down in the market and pointed to a smaller tan-colored fruit, "And what is this?"

Labub answered her, "Those are the Taenah that Sheen mentioned in his example. I could get you one of them if you would like."

Mack smiled at Mike, "Are they also three Ashrah?"

Labub also looked at Mike, but replied, "No, they are only one Ashrah. While just as good tasting as the other two fruit, they are only about one-third the size, therefore assessed the smaller value."

Mack responded before Labub could ask again, "Yes, I would love one, please."

Labub selected one, settled with the shopkeeper, and had Mack sign an entry in his tablet.

That only left Yung, Akilah and Julie without any fruit. Julie, of course, didn't need one.

Nefesh asked Yung if she would like something. She looked at the Taenah, "Sure, I'll have one of those too, please."

Cinam looked at Akilah. Akilah looked at Yung and Mack, who were both smiling and nodding. Akilah then looked further down the stalls and saw another small fruit. She walked quickly to it. It was dark brown, almost black, and roughly the same size as the Taenah.

Akilah asked, "What is that?"

Cinam grinned, "That is my favorite. They are called the Tamareem, but not everyone likes them."

Akilah asked, "Will I like it?"

Cinam shrugged his shoulders, his head cocked to the left.

"I'll have one anyway. They are only one Ashrah also, right?"

Cinam shook his head and held up two fingers.

Akilah questioned, "Why more than a Taenah when they are the same size?"

Cinam almost snorted, "They are special."

Akilah pursed her lips, "Well, so am I. I'll have one please." She looked at Julie.

Julie just shook her head as though thinking, "*Children, children, children,*" but said, "I, of course, do not need to eat. Let's continue our walk."

Cinam signed for Akilah's Tamareem, had her sign for it in Cinam's own tablet, and handed the fruit to her. "Take only a small bite."

Paying him no heed, Akilah took a large bite of the small fruit and began to chew. Immediately her face darkened, she opened her mouth and began fanning it. Cinam had anticipated this and held out a skin of drink he had produced seemingly out of thin air, pulling out the stopper.

Akilah took a long pull from the skin, a deep breath, and whispered, "That is really, really good, but really hot too!"

Cinam added, "I warned you."

Akilah looked down at the ground, "Yes, you did. I'm sorry that I did not do as you asked, but thought I knew better. This is your planet. I should have heeded your judgment." She looked up. There were tears of repentance in her eyes.

Cinam reached out a hand and placed it on her shoulder, "That's okay, lessoned learned. Although I'm not sure why you didn't believe me and needed to learn it as a lesson."

Akilah looked back to the ground, "Me, either."

They all walked out of the market, through the remainder of what appeared to be trees, underground trees, another miracle of this place. There were virtually no buildings or homes, other than Odemel's. Dr. Qxilo asked, "I see no homes. Where do your people live?"

Sheen looked confused again, "Homes?"

Dr. Qxilo rolled his eyes, "Like Odemel's!" He sounded a little too emphatic.

"Oh, that is because he is the Governor. The rest of us just live out of doors." Sheen seem to think that answered it.

"Where do you sleep at night? Do you not have property that you call your own?" There was still an edge to Dr. Qxilo's words.

Sheen squinted, "There is a place where we can rest when we are out by the fields. If that is what you are asking?"

"What if you want to take a rest and you are not out by the fields?" He asked pointedly.

Sheen smiled, "Just lay down and take a rest."

"In the middle of the market," he stated with disdain.

"No, why would you want to lay down in the middle of the market?" Sheen thought that ended it. It seemed to, because Dr. Qxilo gave up his questioning.

They came upon two other buildings.

Mike asked, "Then what are those?" They were very plain. One had smoke coming out of it and the other the whine of some kind of machine.

Keli responded to Mike. "The nearest one, with the smoke, is that of Charash our metal smith, an amazing worker in metals. He and those who work with him have created all the knives you have been using to eat with at Odemel's. He also creates tools and implements that are fitted in the next building. That building houses Allon and all those who work wood with him. Part of it is a mill, hence the sound of machinery that you hear, and then the other part is dedicated to the finer, more detailed aspects of wood working."

It was Akilah's turn to jump in, "Where do you get the wood from?"

Cinam was a little surprised, "From trees of course."

Now it was Akilah's turn to be surprised, "You cut down trees, you kill trees to harvest their wood?'

Cinam looked like she had just slapped him, "No, we don't kill anything. How could you think that?"

Akilah took a deep breath to calm herself, "Then how do you get the wood from the trees?"

Julie spoke up, "Could we go and speak to Nechash and let her tell us her story?"

Cinam looked at the other angels, "Sure, let's do that."

Mike pleaded, "Can we go see the smithy too?"

Keli responded to Mike with, "Yes, we can do that too. Mike, Mack, and Labub, let's go visit Charash. The rest of you go to Nechash's."

Chapter Twenty-Nine
The Smithy

When they walked into Charash's foundry, everyone turned to see the people from Earth and production ground to a halt. Charash stepped from behind the forge. He was covered in an apron of some heavily woven fabric.

"Keli, Labub, to what do I owe the pleasure of your visit? Ah, you have brought some of the Earthlings with you. Welcome to my place of work, although I would call it a labor of love." He was covered in a layer of soot, which was offset by his jovial demeanor.

Keli spoke first, "This is Mike and Mack. They were anxious to see whatever it is that you are working on."

Charash stepped forward to grasp Mike's extended hands, and then lightly kissed the back of Mack's hand. "Please forgive the soot, occupational hazard. Follow me." He took them to a bin filled with a variety of knives. He spoke directly to their minds just as the angels did, also without out need of translation. He pointed, "These are household items, but can you keep a secret?" They both nodded. He took them to his forge and anvil. Across the anvil lay a wondrous-looking sword. He was almost giddy, "I am endeavoring to make a sword for Odemel, like the singing swords of legends that Alathos forged for the archangels before time began."

Mike's eyes grew large as saucers as he looked at the sword, "May I?"

Charash thought for a moment, his head cocked a little to the left, then said, "By all means, but be careful. It is very sharp."

Mike removed his gloves, put them in his spacesuit pocket, and reverently lifted the sword from the anvil. He almost dropped it. It was like touching something living. Its weight and balance were amazing and it simply felt like an extension of his arm. He took a couple of practice swings with it and it actually did sing. Its music was nearly as unnervingly beautiful as its touch. The entire experience was so wonderful that it was difficult to lay it back down and let it go.

"Wow!" Mike exclaimed. "I have never felt anything like that in my life. Does Odemel, as an angel, already have a sword? We always see him with his staff."

Charash smiled, "Ah, the staff of Kadkod. It is also a sword, but this is something entirely different. It is made from a fallen meteor that one of his angels helped me recover from the surface."

Mike still had stars in his eyes, "It is most surely a wonder. Well, your secret is safe with us."

"Now, let me show you something a little more frivolous." He laughed lightly as he took them over to a workbench where one of his people was creating a fine filigree chain. He said to them, "This is Chaleeb." Motioning to the chain, he spoke to Chaleeb, "May I?"

Chaleeb nodded.

Charash motioned for Mack to step forward and turn around. "Can you unzip your suit so that you expose a portion of your neck?"

She did both, stepped forward and unzipped her suit. He lifted the chain off the table, wrapped it around her neck to lay against her skin, and fastened it.

Mack gasped wide-eyed. Just as Mike had never felt anything like the sword, she had never felt anything like this necklace that encircled her neck. It seemed that soft light and liquid love enveloped her. She was having trouble standing. Charash placed a hand on her shoulder to steady her and she was finally able to stand still. She whispered, "Who is the necklace for?"

Charash smiled. "My wife. It, too, is a surprise." He unclasped the necklace and removed it from around her neck.

She turned around, tears in her eyes, reluctant to let it go, feeling like she had just lost something very important. She gave a small bow to Chaleeb, "It truly is also a wonder."

Cinam took Mack's hand. She was still unsteady on her feet. "Let's go join the others in the woodworking building."

Chapter Thirty
The Mill

They joined the others at the mill. It was not operating at the moment, everyone was too mesmerized by the Earthlings. They had been on a tour of the facilities and had just returned, led by Allon to the common area that included some tables and cushions. There were plenty of cushions around the tables, so they all found a place.

Allon continued to stand. "None of this would be possible," and he gestured all around himself, "if it weren't for my wife, Nechash."

She was slightly shorter than he was and broader in the hips. She smiled, perhaps embarrassed.

He addressed her, "Tell them the story," and he added grinning, "please."

Nechash gestured towards the containers and the goblets on the table, "Something to drink?"

She received a chorus of "Please." They lounged around the table, cups were filled, while she and Allon remained standing.

She folded her hands and began reverently, "It was so many years ago," she looked at Allon, "We've lost count. I probably wouldn't remember the incident except it changed the trajectory of my entire life. I was walking through one of our forests. We don't have many, but I came across an unusual tree, two trees perhaps, as it was split down the middle nearly to its base. As I stood there, it spoke to me:

"I am Elah, one of Elohim's first trees. He has a message for you and Odemel will confirm it. You have been given the gift of the language of the trees." The tree paused, "May I also tell you a secret?"

She quickly nodded "*Yes.*"

"You will marry an man named Allon. He will become a great worker in wood, but where will all the wood come from? You will not just chop down trees, that would be murder. However, we will work with you to provide all the wood you need. You will also be sent some others to train in 'whispering to the trees' as we call it. Are you willing?" The tree paused, "Oh, you can breathe now."

She hadn't realized that she had stopped breathing, but she had. She took a slow deep breath. "Why me?"

If a tree could smile, "Let's just say you are 'specialer' than most." and the tree shook her leaves as though laughing.

Nechash took another slow deep breath. "It would be my profound privileged to work with you and your trees." She now addressed those in front of her, "While wood has not been plentiful here, the trees have provided us with enough and for that we are thankful."

Mike took another long drink from his cup, "All of your woodworking is truly amazing. May I ask where your pottery is manufactured?"

"Ah," Allon took a final drink from his cup, "if you'll follow me, I will show you."

They all took a final drink and arose from their cushions.

They walked slowly through the shop and past the machinery, which only half of them had seen before. Out the back of the building stood a much smaller building. Inside were four potter's wheels, but only one was occupied. They walked up to it and Allon introduced, "This is Jevan, excuse him for not rising to greet you. He can't get up in the middle of a throwing or he will lose his precious rhythm."

He did slow down his peddling as he realized they were the Earthlings. "Welcome to my shop. I hope Allon hasn't been boring you with too many woodland tales."

They both laughed.

Mike asked, "Is all the pottery cast and fired here?"

"Yes," Jevan answered, "although I often have three apprentices assisting me, when Allon hasn't conscripted them to carry wood for him."

More laughter between the two of them. There was a tray of cups off to Jevan's side, but within reach.

Jevan pointed, added, "Ready for the kiln in the morning."

Mike asked again, "You don't paint them before you fire them?"

Jevan scrunched up his brows. "Why would I do that?"

"To make a set or a cup individually unique, more special to the recipient," Mike elaborated.

"Hmmm, what an interesting idea. I'll have to give it some thought. Thanks for stopping by Earthlings." He turned his full attention back to the wheel.

Odemel turned first. "Back outside and to the fields."

The others followed.

Chapter Thirty-One
Fields White unto Harvest

Each field was full of a variety of fruit. The Taenah grew on the ground, the Inveem and Anavaheem in small bushes, and the Tamareem in trees. The fields were separated into small patches supporting each different kind of fruit, all distinct, and each the product of obvious care.

The next question came from Dr. Qxilo, "Tell me about the ownership of the fields."

"Most of the Haklayeem, you would call them farmers, have been working with these crops for thousands of years. They have a cooperative relationship with them, the plants and their produce. They take care of each other. The individual Haklah takes care of a specific plant to help it grow, and the plant produces fruit to feed the Haklah. It is a mutually beneficial relationship. It is the same between the Haklayeem. It is not a competition. All the Haklayeem who work with Anavaheem do so together, using similar, if not identical, methods. There is no haggling over prices, everyone knows the value of the Anavaheem. It is three

Ashrah. Wherever you purchase one it is always three Ashrah. Does that answer your question?"

Mike required some clarification. "Do each of the Haklayeem own the same amount of crops?"

Keli answered him as they all continued to walk among the fields, "Relatively so, based on the expected output or harvest of their crop each year. It would appear that the owner of a Taenah plot would have a plot about three times larger than the owner of a plot of Inveem. You must remember that we have been doing this for thousands of years, but it has all worked out to be about equal, based on the value of the product and its yield per plot size, per year."

Dr. Qxilo chimed back in, "And there is no competition between farmers to see who could produce the most?"

Sheen looked puzzled again, "Why would we want to do that? We all have more than enough. We are content with what we have and with what we can obtain if needed."

Dr. Qxilo went on, "What of poverty?"

Sheen still looked puzzled, "Of what?"

Dr. Qxilo seemed almost angry, "Poverty, poverty, what of poverty?"

Sheen shook his head, "I'm sorry, I do not know that word. What does it mean?"

The doctor spat out the words, "What of those who have nothing, those who lack what the others have?"

Sheen squinted, "There is no one like that here."

Dr. Qxilo *Humphed!* and stomped off ahead.

Sheen looked at the others, "What is the matter with the doctor?"

Yung tried to cover for him, "He's okay, he's just confused and doesn't understand how there can be a society and culture without poverty or competition."

They walked in silence for a bit. It was particularly unsettling to be in an underground realm of light, peace, and alien beauty. They walked until they came to a crossroads, complete with a roundabout. The roads to the right and the left went off to what must be Martian living areas. Coming from one was a large cart or wagon, pulled by a large beast that might be the Martian approximation of a horse, with two Martians riding on the wagon. There was also a small animal running ahead of it, the cross between a sheep and a dog. Mike knelt down and held out a hand as it approached. It was unafraid and loped right up to him to enthusiastically lick his hand. Mike petted it and it walked right up and into his embrace, nearly knocking him over in its playfulness. Mike was laughing and having a grand old time as the wagon approached.

Odemel called out to them. "Darah and Darmah, these are our visitors from the Dark world."

Darah addressed them, "A pleasure to meet you. We are on the way to the market with some of our Rimon." The visitors gathered around and looked in the cart to find round dark fruit, the size of a large fist. "Would you like some?"

Mike asked, "How much are they?"

Darmah smiled, "They would be our gift to you, a gesture of good will between our races."

Mack spoke with little hesitation, "And what may we offer you in return?"

Darah answered, "The pledge of your friendship would be enough."

Mike reached over and picked one up and proclaimed, "Done!" They each picked one up, all except the doctor. Mike questioned, "Doctor?"

"Not hungry, thank you," he replied, although it seemed like a rebuff.

Darah and Darnah looked at one another, then Darnah called out, "Have a good day," and Darah made a clicking sound that caused the beast to begin pulling the wagon again. Mike gave a final pet to the small animal and off it ran with them.

Yung questioned Dr. Qxilo, "Don't you think you should have taken one, even if you weren't going to eat it right now?"

He spat back, "I wasn't hungry!"

They all stood there at the roundabout, stunned by Dr. Qxilo's behavior.

Odemel spoke up, "Perhaps it's time for you to go back to your compound?"

Some of them looked at one another, while some of them looked at the ground.

"Please take the hand of your companion angel."

Even those who had been looking down, looked up and took their angel's hand, except Dr. Qxilo. Sheen reached out and placed a hand on his shoulder and before he had time to shrug it off, they were all transported back to the colony's compound. They said quick goodbyes to their angel companions who disappeared in the blink of an eye.

Chapter Thirty-Two
The Darkness Dawns

It had began as such a small thing. When Dr. Qxilo had been awakened on the voyage to Mars, he liked his tea with two spoonfuls of sugar. He began drinking his tea that way as a private celebration of the day they handed him his doctor certification and he knew that he would never have to go back to being poor again. Unfortunately, aboard ship, they were each rationed to only one spoonful. Rather than negotiate with someone who didn't put sugar in their tea, which might have been embarrassing, he began to take extra and store it in his quarters. If he would have thought about it, he would have realized that Julie had eyes all over the ship. She knew, but did not feel it was time to confront him. Besides, Yung didn't use any sugar in her tea. Dr. Qxilo may have thought himself above the rules for in China doctors were revered and people expected them to do whatever they wanted. If he had thought about it, he might have recognized a persistent underlying frustration at being treated as only an equal to the rest of the crew. However, he did not think about it. He just took the extra sugar as if it was owed him.

They sat around the dinner table.

Yung was still curious, "Doctor, why did you not take one of the Rimon? You didn't see it as a possible affront to our friendship with the Martians?"

Dr. Qxilo sighed, but it resembled a *"humph."* "I do not like being forced to do something and it seemed forced to me. If I want to extend my friendship, I will do it on my own terms."

"Still…" and she left the sentence hanging.

"What do you think, Julie?" Mike asked.

Julie smiled her usual smile, "This is all uncharted territory for us. Even I, with my access to nearly infinite data, can only approximate the future, not predict it."

"And your approximation in this case?" Mike continued his line of questioning.

"My best estimate is that they will extend the good doctor the grace to believe that he truly didn't take a Rimon because he was not hungry and that they will not impute anything else to his reason for refusing the offer."

With that they moved on to other things.

Later that week, Yung was in the shower, having just soaped herself all over, including her hair, when she felt a blast of cold air. She washed the suds out of her eyes and turned to find Dr. Qxilo standing there. She covered the appropriate areas with her hands as she exclaimed, "What are you doing here?"

He just stood there looking at her, no attempt to avert his eyes, "Taking a shower."

She tried covering herself with the spray of the water too. "This time is reserved for us women."

"I needed a shower," he demanded. "Why should I wait. Just turn around, you'll be fine. I'll use the shower head over here," and he turned his back on her.

She stood there a moment until he looked over his shoulder to see her again. She finished rinsing and left the bath chamber.

Wrapped in her towel, she went directly to Akilah's quarters. She knocked.

Akilah called out, "Come in."

Yung was furious and stomped through the doorway.

"What's the matter?"

"Dr. Qxilo just walked in while I was taking my shower. His disdain for rules is becoming a problem. I think we need to bring this up to the entire crew. What do you think?"

Akilah looked off to the left, over Yung's head. "I think we need to be very careful. This could break the team apart. We need to plan for the best time to do this, but you are right. We must do something and soon."

They had agreed to invite their companion angels to their compound for supper. Even though angels did not need to eat, they could. After supper they took the angels on a tour of the facilities. They split up to tour the garden domes.

While Dr. Qxilo and Sheen were in the fruit dome, the doctor surreptitiously picked some berries and put them into a pouch. He thought to himself, "*These will never be missed.*" He gave the bag to Sheen.

"I would like you to do me a favor. The couple of workers who we met on the road, whose Rimon I did not eat, could you give these berries to them? I know Julie said it was not perceived as a lapse of etiquette on my part? But just in case it might have been, this might make up for it. Oh, I would also appreciate it if you could keep this just between the two of us."

Sheen looked at him with a strange expression, wondering, *"Why the secrecy?"* but put the pouch in a pocket of his robe and agreed that he would do so at his earliest opportunity.

Dr. Qxilo thanked him.

Chapter Thirty-Three
Berry Troubling

Darah and Darnah stood at the counter where they prepared meals. They had before them the pouch of berries from Dr. Qxilo that Sheen had given them. He had said it was to make up for any possible offense they had felt by the doctor not having accepted their gift of a Rimon. They had not taken offense, why should they? Yet, they now had this pouch of berries, had no idea what to do with it, and no one knew that they had it. Sheen had given it to them shrouded in some kind of secrecy. They were not sure why. It just was what it was.

They decided to mash up the berries, mix it with some hot water and drink it. It proved just the right balance of sweetness and tartness. It made almost two liters of hot drink, but the two of them took their time, and that evening finished off the entire two liters.

Sheen revisited the couple later that evening and found them on the ground near their wagon making funny noises and acting silly. While he was there, they both passed out. Worried, Sheen called out to Odemel, who stepped out of a portal next to them all. He knelt down and checked out the couple thoroughly. When Odemel asked what Sheen had witnessed, Sheen described their funny sounds and silly antics.

"Did you notice anything else unusual?" Odemel inquired of Sheen.

Sheen then told him of the pouch of berries that Dr. Qxilo had asked him to give the couple in secret. They went into the dining area and found the empty pouch, the bowl the berries had been crushed in, and the container that had contained the hot drink. Odemel smelled the container and tasted some of the residue.

"Hmmm, I think this is what happened. These alien berries, having been drunk by Darah and Darnah, when digested, have caused the unusual behavior and what now passes for sleeping. I need to go have a chat with our alien friends."

Julie felt Odemel's words forming in her mind, "Could you come outside the ship? I need to speak with you."

She formed the words in her own mind, "I will be right there." On her way to the airlock, she passed Yung, "I need to go outside for a few minutes." She stepped into the airlock to initiate the process of its operation.

Once outside, she walked around the corner of the building and there stood Odemel. She bowed her head slightly and said, "Odemel?"

He came directly to the point. "It seems that Dr. Qxilo has given some berries from Earth to Sheen to give to Darah and Darnah. They made the berries into a drink and had an allergic reaction that resembles your intoxication. Sheen later found them acting silly on the floor and then they passed out on the ground. Concerned, he called me. My subjects, the Ma-adeem, have never encountered anything like this before. While, I do not think that Dr.Qxilo realized that this would happen. Even so, before any more food is exchanged between your people and mine, I strongly suggest you and I talk about it first."

Concerned, Julie asked, "Will your people be okay?"

Odemel smiled, "Yes, and I will take steps to assure that they do not remember what happened."

Julie continued, "and you can rest assured that we will talk about this as a team tonight."

He reached out a hand, she took it in both of her own and touched it to her forehead. "I'm sorry this has happened."

He took his hand back, "No worries, all will be well."

That night after supper, Julie broached the subject, "Dr. Qxilo, it has come to my attention that you gave some berries from Earth to Sheen to deliver to the Martians we met taking their wagon of Rimon to the market."

Dr. Qxilo stammered, "What….who told you this?"

Julie went on, "They had an allergic reaction to those berries that resembled intoxication, something that has never happened before on this planet."

He still stuttered, "What, how could I know that would happen?"

Julie continued, "What made you think that you had the right to do that at all, Doctor?"

Now the doctor bristled, "I was trying to be proactive, to right the potential wrong I did by not eating their Rimon fruit."

"That, Doctor, was particularly irresponsible for you, especially as a doctor. We have no idea what our food may do to the aliens on this planet. We were warned that they were concerned about the evil we might bring from our darkened world. Now, you have introduced two of them to that evil darkness."

"What?" he exclaimed, "how could an allergic reaction resembling intoxication be considered an evil brought from our dark planet?"

"Doctor, have you no sense of history? Do you not know of the destruction of indigenous peoples who had no way to battle the diseases that foreigners brought with them? In this ideal paradise we have no way of knowing what eating the food from our darkened planet will do to them."

Dr. Qxilo looked down at the table, "I guess I didn't think it through."

"Why did you act on your own, without consulting the rest of us? Why?" Julie's questions were pointed.

Yung spoke up, "Because he thinks that he is better than the rest of us." She then said sarcastically, "He's a doctor after all, not a mere mortal like us." She went on, "He thinks he is above the rules. Why, this morning he entered the shower while I was taking mine. When I told him it was the women's shower time, he said that he wanted a shower and proceeded to shower anyway. 'Just turn your back, it won't matter.' he said. Well, it did matter! I felt violated, exposed, dirty, and I had done nothing wrong."

"Is this true?" Julie confronted him.

He looked them all straight in the face, "Well, it is an absurd rule."

"Not to the women," Julie countered. She felt it was time, "And what about the sugar that you have been stealing?"

He looked like he'd been slapped, "What?"

"We have each been allowed a spoonful of sugar for our coffee or tea, but you want two, so you have been stealing it and keeping it in your cabin."

The doctor shot back, accusingly, "I thought you didn't have cameras in the crew quarters!"

"That is true, but I have them everywhere else. I have seen you steal it and take it back to your quarters. I don't need to know exactly where you are stashing it."

The doctor looked back down at the table, seemingly ashamed.

Yung spoke compassionately now, "I don't take sugar in my tea. Why didn't you just ask for my allotment?"

Still looking at the table he answered almost too quietly to be heard, "But that would make me…." He couldn't even finish the sentence.

"Dependent?" Yung interjected softly. "There is nothing weak or wrong about us being interdependent with each other. We are supposed to be a team. That is how this mission, this colony was designed to operate, but you have violated our trust again and again by acting independently." There were now tears in Yung's eyes.

Dr. Qxilo looked up a little, barely able to meet their eyes, and swallowed hard. "How do I regain your trust?" he asked slowly.

They all looked at Julie, and Yung asked, "Julie?"

Julie's response was slow and measured. "The core foundation of walking with Jesus is repentance. It is much more than just being sorry. It is being sorry enough to change your belief and your behavior. Doctor, do you believe that you are better than the rest of us?"

He was back to looking at the table. "As a doctor, yes, but as a pilot, mechanic, botanist, or psychiatrist, no."

"And as a person?"

Dr. Qxilo began to realize that he had thought his status as a doctor made him a better person, more valuable than the rest of them. "I must confess that as a doctor I did see myself as having more value than the rest of you." Tears now glistened in his eyes. "I was wrong. I ask you to please forgive me." He actually began to sob, "Forgive me for the sugar, the shower, the berries, but even more so for the fundamental error in my valuation of each and everyone of you." He put his head in his hands and wept openly.

Yung was the first to get up, walk over, put a hand on his shoulder and say, "I forgive you."

She was followed by each of the others each doing the same, including, last of all, Julie.

Chapter Thirty-Four
Restored

The next few days, things seemed to have returned to normal. The crew went about its chores in a mood that bordered on cheerful.

Julie felt Odemel call her outside again. She excused herself and went outside. Rounding the corner, there he stood.

He simply asked, "Well?"

Julie sighed, "Dr. Qxilo has confessed, repented, been forgiven, and I think things have returned to a state of normalcy. What about on your end?"

Odemel smiled slightly, "Darah and Darnah have also returned to normal, with no recollection of the incident. Perhaps we can look on the bright side of the events and appreciate the outcome, regardless of the journey to get there."

"What do you see as next?" Julie asked.

"Could you send Akilah out to speak with me?"

Julie was surprised, "Can't you just speak with her personally and call her out here yourself?"

His smile lingered, "I could, but I believe it would be better coming through you."

Julie gave him a quick nod, "Okay," and turned to go.

Odemel spoke to her back, "Thank you."

She replied over her shoulder, "You're welcome."

Julie found Akilah in her quarters reading. "Odemel would like to speak with you outside."

She jumped up and closed her book with an, "Okay, thanks."she grabbed her helmet and gloves from her quarters, and her rebreathing unit on the way to the airlock. Outside and around the corner she met Odemel.

"You wanted to speak with me?" Then she added, "You don't really need to be standing in front of me to speak to me, do you?"

He smiled, "It is more honoring to our relationship to do it this way. Is it okay if we go to my home?"

"Just let me tell Julie." She called to Julie, "I'm going to Odemel's home for a bit. I'll keep you posted." She turned to Odemel, "Okay," and took his offered hand. She found herself in his courtyard, "Why not in your home?" She questioned.

"Materializing out of thin air inside my home might be rather disconcerting to the help," he explained.

"Can't you tell if anyone is going to be there before you 'land' so to speak?" It seemed like a logical question.

"More or less, yes, but the odds of someone not being there are significantly better here in the courtyard," he clarified.

She sighed, "So, why have you brought me here to your home?"

He looked over her head to the right, "I wanted to have a private discussion and it seemed it would be easier here."

They went into the house and walked to the sitting room, meeting a serving angel along the way. "My Lord, should I get some water for her feet?"

Odemel looked at Akilah.

"I'm fine, but thank you for the thought. I still feel very welcomed from last time," she told the angel. "By the way, I don't think I caught your name?"

He laughed under his breath, "I didn't realize that you were seeking to catch it. Let me simplify things. I am called Rukhot. It may be because some find me 'full of hot air.'" His laughter rang-out.

"Ah, a pleasure to formally meet you, Rukhot," and she held out her hand.

He looked at Odemel, who nodded almost imperceptibly. He reached out and took her hand to lightly kiss its back. "The pleasure is all mine, I assure you."

Odemel spoke to Rukhot, "Would you bring us some Anavaheem juice, please?"

Rukhot bowed slightly. "Certainly," he replied and left the sitting room.

Odemel motioned Akilah to a cushion and she sat down, looking around almost apprehensively. He spoke, "Everything is okay, I just want to talk to you. Actually, I have a proposition for you. How would you like to live here with me?"

Akilah smiled slyly, "You're suggesting we move in together? You want to marry me?"

Odemel laughed outright, then paused. "No, that has been tried before. They were Fallen angels, but it resulted in the abominations called the Ashareem. No, I do not want you to be my wife, but I do want you to live here as the ambassador between our two peoples."

Akilah wasn't sure if she were sad or relieved. "I know that you mentioned that before, but most of your conversations have begun through Julie. Would she be a better representative?"

"Ah…" intoned Odemel, "I like Julie, but she is not human. Sentient, but not human. It would be much more appropriate if you would do me the honor."

Akilah was touched and honored at the thought of acting as the Martian ambassador. "I would live here with you?"

"If that would seem appropriate, yes." He, too, seemed truly pleased.

"Would it be all right if I talked about it with Julie first?" she asked.

He smiled, "See, you are already acting like an ambassador. Yes, that would be fine. By all means consult Julie on the matter. Now, how about some supper?"

She nodded, "*Yes,*" and he began to ask her questions about her life, growing up, and aspirations as a Martian colonist.

Chapter Thirty-Five
Moving Day

When Akilah returned to the compound, she immediately sought out Julie and asked her about Odemel's offer. Julie thought it was a great idea and mentioned that she wished she were human so that she could have been in the running for the position. Akilah was secretly glad she hadn't been. She wasn't sure she would have been offered the position if it had been a level playing field.

The next morning at breakfast Akilah informed the rest of the team that she would be moving in with Odemel to become the official ambassador between the races of the Earthlings and the Martians. Everyone seemed pleased with the arrangement, although Julie noticed that Dr. Qxilo had been looking away or down at his hands during most of her announcement. Yung followed her to her quarters to help her pack. She didn't have much, so they were done quickly. Yung gave her a hug and she left without any other fanfare.

Cinam awaited her outside the compound. "I was very glad to hear that you will be moving into the city with us."

Akilah thought to herself, "*It's really only a town compared to what we would call a city.*" Out loud she asked, "Are there other cities on the planet?"

Cinam smiled, "Oh, yes, but this is the capital because Odemel lives here."

"*That would make sense,*" she also thought to herself.

Cinam took her and her bag to Odemel's and showed her the room that would be hers. It was not opulent, but it was quite nice. It had a cushion bed, a cupboard for her clothes, and a writing desk. A doorway off to the back led to a place where she could bathe. If you considered a basin, washcloth, and towel a bath. Then there was a covered bucket she assumed was her toilet. Knowing the premium the Martians placed on water, she asked Cinam, "Do I have an allotment of water?"

He looked at her questioningly, "Yes, but because you are the ambassador it really doesn't apply, besides, all of the water is reclaimed, processed, and reused."

She was going to ask him, "There are no doors, what if I want some privacy?" but realized that with no shame there was no need for privacy. What she did ask was, "What if I want some time alone?"

"No one will ever enter your room, except to clean it when you are occupied elsewhere, or if you ask them to come into your room." He said forthrightly.

"There are no doors," she stated.

He looked up, confused, "Why would you need a door?" He acted like the question made no sense.

"What if I want to change my clothes?" she suggested.

Cinam chuckled, "We don't wear clothes. If you want to change your clothes, just change them."

She sighed and thought again, "*This is going to take some getting used to, but it will be a refreshing change for the good. I guess I could just turn my back towards the door in the off chance someone walked by.*"

Cinam smiled, "Take some time settling in. Someone will come to collect you for lunch."

"And if I'd like to go for a walk?" She cocked her head to the left.

"Just call for me. I should probably accompany you for a while, until the novelty of 'an Earthling in our midst' wears off." He was now stifling another chuckle. He gave her a little wave as he walked off. He was rather likable and she was very glad that he had been selected to be her angelic companion.

She placed her folded clothing in her cupboard. She realized that she didn't need much since the Ma-adeem wore no clothes at all, except like the smitty's apron for protection. She began contemplating going around 'in the buff' as none of the Ma-adeem would care. "*Hmmm, what an interesting idea.*" She sorted the rest of her few things and found places for them. She didn't have that much. She walked over and sat at her desk. She found a three ring binder of golden plates. They probably weren't gold, but appeared to be a soft and golden metal, along with what looked like a steel stylus. She moved the plates in front of her. At the top of the first plate was embossed, "Akilah from Earth" and a short note of welcome from Odemel.

Welcome Akilah,
I hope that this assignment will come to you as a pleasure and not just a duty. You may wonder how I could prepare this for you in advance. Did

I know you would accept my proposal? You must remember that I am an angel and who it is that I serve. I do not have foreknowledge, but he may share with me what he wills. He assured me that there was a good chance that you would accept, so I prepared this. I believe that you will serve both of our races very well and I look forward to working with you for a long time.

Your Friend,
Governor Odemel

Akilah found that she had tears in her eyes when she finished reading it. She began to score the soft metal,

"*Today is my first formal day as the ambassador between the peoples of Earth and those of Mars.*"

She had filled most of the page when someone called to her to announce lunch. She stated, "I'll be right there." When she met the angel, she realized that it was not Rukhot. "You are not Rukhot, but we met at the foot washing my first time here. May I know your name?"

He seemed surprised that she felt she needed his permission, "I am called Nobah."

She held out her hand, "My pleasure to meet you."

He brought her hand to his lips and lightly kissed the back of it, "My pleasure. Lunch?" and he gestured with his hand towards the dining area.

She followed him there, The table was set with a number of dishes she didn't recognize.

Odemel stood at the head of the table, "Would you like to ask him to bless our food and time together?"

"I would very much like to," and she looked to the empty place at the other end of the table, "Thank you for allowing us to come to Mahdeem. Help us to bring only light and no darkness at all, and thank you for all of this which I cannot begin to describe." She looked back to Odemel and he gestured for them to be seated.

Chapter Thirty-Six
The Others

Odemel began to explain some of the food that was on the table, "You will recognize some of the fruit on the table: Inveem, Taenah, Anavaheeem, and Rimon. The cooked vegetables you have not seen yet. We do eat some vegetables raw, like we do the fruit, but some of them are also quite good when cooked. For instance, the Carpon," and he pointed, "the Beza-bezel," and he pointed at it, "and the Notair. If you are to try all three, I would suggest you eat the Beza-bezel as the middle course."

She nodded to Nobah who was serving them and he put all three on her plate. The Carpon reminded her of cooked carrot, the Beza-bezel was hot like a pepper, and Notair resembled a cauliflower. They were all quite good, especially when washed down with the fruity drink provided.

Odemel interjected, "I have taken the liberty of also inviting a few notable individuals who I want you to get to know in your new position."

His timing was impeccable as Rukhot stepped into the doorway and introduced the first one, "Azbon has arrived."

Odemel was surprised to see Akilah put down her knife, wipe her hands, and arise from the table. It was obvious that Azbon was also surprised.

Before either of them spoke, she held out her hand, "Azbon, I am called Akilah, from Earth, obviously."

Azbon looked quickly at Odemel, afraid of making an error of etiquette, but Odemel just smiled and nodded slightly. Azbon took her hand, brought it to his lips, lightly kissed it, and said, "My pleasure."

Odemel motioned him to a seat and he sat. Azbon lifted his goblet which Nobah was quick to fill.

Odemel added, "Azbon is the head of our marketplace, in charge of the stalls, their setup and clean up, arrangement, and assignment, and as you have witnessed, he is exceptional at doing all of these tasks."

Azbon turned away, he might have been blushing at the compliment.

Now reseated, Akilah spoke to Azbon, "I would agree with Odemel. Your market is a wonder of beauty and order, in stark contrast to the chaos that is called a marketplace on my planet."

He smiled at the compliment. Although unsure he knew what she meant by chaos, he did not turn away as he had with Odemel's compliment.

Ruhkot stood in the doorway with an angel this time, "Makael has arrived." Almost following Akilah's lead, they all stood to welcome Makael.

Akilah stepped foward slightly, her hand outstretched, "Akilah of Earth."

Makael did not even look at Odemel, but stepped smartly forward in a military manner, took her hand and lightly kissed it, stepped back as he clicked his heels together and pronounced, 'Makael' with a slight bow of the head.

"Makael," Odemel stated perfunctorily, "is the head of my angelic forces here on Mahdeem. You might consider him a lieutenant."

Akilah looked to Odemel, "Do you need non-angelic military forces here?"

Odemel chuckled, "Of course not, and Makael's function here is not military in nature, but more administrative of personnel and assignments. He does report directly to me."

Makael nodded. Nobah handed him a filled goblet also, and they all sat, too quickly it would seem, as Rukhot stood at the doorway again.

"Ginnethon," he announced.

They scrambled to their feet, following Akilah again. Ginnethon nodded at each of them and then realized Akilah had held out her hand.

As he took it, she announced, "Akilah," and chuckled, "from Earth," as if there was any question.

He lightly kissed the back of her hand and then produced a flower he had been holding behind his back, "Welcome." While not being an angel, Ginnethon was suave in his own right.

"He is the head of agriculture here," Odemel elaborated.

It was Akilah's turn to blush, "Why thank you, Ginnethon." She turned to Odemel, "Do you have a container I could put this in?" She looked back to Ginnethon, who now held out a pottery vase he had seemingly produced from thin air. It was even filled with water. His thoughtfulness touched her deeply and she warmed to him immediately. She could hardly speak, although because they were speaking mentally, it was passed to him, yet in a whisper. This mental language was interesting. It was very similar to spoken language. If you wanted to speak to multiple people, it was broadcast to them. If you wanted to keep it private, it was private. It intrigued her. So much of communication depended on the intent of the heart.

There were still two empty plates at the table. One always remained empty, but she wondered who the final one was for. She did not need to wonder long. Rukhot appeared again to announce, "Charash," and another Ma-adeem crossed the threshold.

She had not sat, only placed the vase on the table and wiped her eyes. She blinked twice and held out her hand, "Akilah of Earth."

He smiled quite broadly, "I would have never guessed." He took her offered hand, brought it to his lips, and lightly kissed it, "My pleasure. I have a gift for you. Odemel does not know I have done this and for that I ask his pardon." Without releasing her hand, he reached into his robe and brought out an intricately woven bracelet of silver metallic threads reflecting the soft light. Charash spread the bracelet around her wrist and fastened some invisible clasp.

"How can I ever thank you?" She barely got out the words.

His smile broadened, "I have it on the best authority that you will surely try," and he actually winked at Odemel.

"Charash is a jewelry smith, among having other talents. Mike and Mack met him the other day, but you were in theater building." Odemel chuckled. He gestured for them to all sit.

Odemel took the lead. "I have brought you here, besides to consume my food and drink, to get to know Akilah. She will be our ambassador to the Earthlings. Initially, I would like all of your contact with them to be initiated through her. They will not walk through our town and countryside unattended."

Makael spoke, "Is that for our protection or theirs?"

Odemel squinted, "How would they be unprotected in our midst?"

Makael looked away, "As a novelty they might be approached unwontedly."

Odemel shrugged, "Ah, yes, This is all uncharted territory here, dealing with the Darkened."

Akilah was a bit taken back, "We are all to be considered 'darkened'?" She found the word vaguely offensive, especially as they were using it.

Odemel sighed, "I'm sorry if I overgeneralize, but you are from the only dark planet there has ever been. Your darkness may be contagious. We do not know, but it is in our best interest to be prudent."

"Yes," she agreed reluctantly, "it probably is." She looked up at him.

He sighed again, "Thank you, I knew you were the right person for this job."

They continued their discussions which were centered around getting to know Akilah and being able to trust her. They were surprised on every level, until they found it difficult to look at her as one of the 'darkened', but rather to be trusted as one of their own. Again, it was all Odemel had hoped for.

Chapter Thirty-Seven
The Darkened

Odemel presented her the next morning with a ruby pendant. The chain was made of the soft silvery material that she now recognized.

"May I put it on you?" he requested.

She turned around for him to do so. He unclasped it, and placed both ends in one hand which he held in front of her. He reached around her with the other hand, took one of the clasps in that hand and brought the necklace and pendant back until it lay between her breasts. She had unzipped her suit, so that it actually did lay between her breasts. He stepped close to her as he redid the clasps. It seemed a gesture of intimacy.

Akilah found she had been holding her breath.

He placed his hands on her shoulders and turned her around.

She began to stammer, "Thank you….it's…"

He finished her sentence, "It is the Kadkod, the same material as the gem on my staff. In fact, it is a shard from that same gem."

She found that she couldn't speak again.

He continued, "It will allow you to pass into my city unassisted. However, I would ask that for a time you continue to allow Cinam to accompany you."

Her stammer continued, "How can I….."

He smiled, "I'm sure that you will prove worthy of it many times over. I have that faith in you. You'll also notice that it is thin enough to be virtually unnoticeable under your suit. When asked about it, say that it is a gift commensurate with your new office as ambassador, which is also true. Now, if you'd like to go back to your compound and convey to your people the substance of our first meeting, Cinam is here."

She nodded in the affirmative and Odemel walked away to be replaced by Cinam.

She had zipped up her suit and held her hand over where the pendant still lay between her breasts. It was softly warm and brought a smile to her face. She put on her gloves, helmet, and rebreather,

Cinam looked at her, "He gave you the Kadkod?"

She smiled deeply, "You knew?"

He looked down, "Yes, he said you would eventually be able to pass without me."

"But it doesn't mean I have to, or want to."

He struggled to understand, "Really, why not?"

She continued, "Because I like being with you, Cinam."

He smiled, "and I really like being with you," then he said smartly, "So, for now," and he reached out a hand. She grasped it and they immediately appeared a short ways from the compound. "I will teach you how to use it," and he squeezed her hand, "later." She let go and he was gone. She remembered the first times that they had transferred, there was a rumble and a flash of light. Now, it seemed as normal as blinking your eyes.

She announced herself to Julie, "May I have a chat with the team?"

Julie responded, "Sure, we are still sitting around the breakfast table."

Akilah entered and they were all seated in their usual seats. Mike got up and bowed slightly, "Welcome back, Ambassador." He said it with a straight face, but there was a grin in there somewhere.

Dr. Qxilo seemed bored, "Well?"

Akilah addressed Julie, "Do you know that they refer to us as 'the Darkened'?"

Julie looked around the table, "It seems appropriate since we come from the only dark planet. We have known since the onset that they are worried that our darkness might follow us like a contagion."

Akilah looked especially at Dr. Qxilo, "A worry that we have not dispelled, but probably reinforced."

The doctor lashed out "I thought I was forgiven?"

"That is not the same as forgotten. It remains a wrong that we have not made right," Akilah replied.

He looked at the table, "I was only trying…." and left the words hanging.

"And we know that you are truly sorry. Yet the fact remains, that the burden of repairing the lost trust with the angels remains yours," Yung weighed in.

"And unfortunately, that blight passes to us all. You will continue to need to be accompanied at all times while you are in Haechad, Odemel's city, and its surrounding fields and farm land. I have met with some of the town's leaders, though: the head of his armies, his director of agriculture, the market director, and a jewelry smith." She held out her wrist. "The smithy gave me this." The bracelet sparkled even in the ship's subdued lighting.

Yung bent over it admiringly, "Wow, it is beautiful. What is it made of?"

"Some native metal filigree," Akilah responded. "Do you have any questions?"

They continued to chat for the next hour.

When they were through, Akilah spoke almost gravely, "I should be getting back. They would like to plan a celebration welcoming you all formally to their planet."

Yung asked, "Can I go back with you now?"

"I will ask, but I would think that it is okay."

Mike jumped in with, "I have a pair of binoculars I can part with that they might find interesting. Could I send them back with you?"

Akilah was pleased, "I will ask about that also. Let me go outside and speak with Cinam."

They nodded, she donned her gloves, helmet, and rebreather and headed for the airlock.

Chapter Thirty-Eight
A Gift in Return

Outside, Akilah found Cinam waiting. She asked, "Would it be all right if Yung came back with us?"

He nodded.

"And Mike would like to send a gift, a pair of binoculars. You look through them and the image of what you are looking at is enlarged."

He nodded again.

"Who should I present the binoculars to?" she asked.

"Why me, of course," and he laughed, then added, "Makael would be quite pleased with that gift."

"Great! I'll go get Yung and the binoculars."

"And I will have Nefesh meet us."

When Akilah and Yung came back outside, both Cinam and Nefesh were standing there, each with a hand outstretched. They took their hands and found themselves in Odemel's courtyard.

"Is this the only spot we can transfer to?" Yung inquired.

Nefesh responded, "Of course not. It is just the easiest."

They took off their helmets and gloves, and put them in their pockets. Akilah mentioned, "Is there any reason that we need to meet you outside of the ship to be transferred here?

Cinam and Nefesh looked at each other and shrugged their shoulders.

"If you met us in the airlock we wouldn't need to take our helmets, gloves, and rebreathers on every trip."

"That would be fine with us, but we would need your permission to enter your ship" Cinam announced.

Akilah looked off to the side, "I will talk about it with my people."

Odemel stood at his front door and motioned for them to come in. This time Rukhot and Nobah were prepared with water for their feet. The washing and blessing was just as impactful as the first time and both Akilah and Yung had tears in their eyes as they were led into Odemel's sitting room.

Before she sat, Yung announced, "I have a present for the leader of your angel armies."

Odemel turned back to the doorway as Rukhot announced, "Makael."

Odemel gestured towards Yung, "Makael, this is Yung, she has a gift for you."

Makael bowed and Yung stepped forward and held out a bag, which she opened and, from it, removed the binoculars. "This is a device to aid you in your looking far away. When you hold it up to your eyes," and she demonstrated, "that which is far away, appears to be near." She reached out to hand it to him. He bowed again as he accepted it.

He turned to look back out the doorway as he lifted it to his eyes. He was so startled that he almost dropped it, as he exclaimed, "What?" He lifted it again to his eyes, "Is this some kind of mystery?"

Yung smiled, "No, just artful engineering and craftsmanship. Your smith will be impressed also, I'm sure."

And with those words barely spoken, Charash stood there. Makael handed the binoculars to him and gestured that he should put them to his eyes as he looked out into the courtyard. He, too, nearly dropped them as he exclaimed, "What?"

Yung simply stated, " A gift from us to you. I hope you can share them or perhaps have our engineer teach you how to replicate them."

Charash spoke to Akilah, "Is that even possible?"

She smiled broadly. "Perhaps," and she paused, "...we'll have to see."

Akilah turned back to Odemel, "Yung's specialty is the relationships between people. I was wondering if she and Nefesh could spend the day interacting with some of the locals, if her asking a lot of questions would not be too much of an imposition to them and their activities?"

Odemel's endearing smile returned, "I'm sure most of the Ma-adeem would willingly drop whatever it is that they are doing for the opportunity to speak with an Earthling. Wouldn't you agree, Nefesh?"

Nefesh bowed slightly, "Yes, they would most willingly. I'm afraid that she may be overwhelmed with questions herself." He turned to Yung, "You will be quite a novelty."

Odemel sugested, "Let's meet back here for lunch."

They all agreed.

Nefesh and Yung had an amazing time. He started in the marketplace where she interviewed some of the different vendors. Then they went and met Atulah. Her husband was out working in the field, but would be back for lunch. Unfortunately, they wouldn't be able to stay to meet him, but Yung still had plenty of questions for Atulah.

Yung asked, "How does your husband display his anger and frustration?"

Atulah looked at her like she didn't understand, "Anger?"

"Yes, when you have different opinions and can't come to a mutually agreed upon conclusion," she explained.

Atulah smiled, "If we haven't agreed, then we aren't done talking."

Yung tried again, "Who usually wins the discussion when you disagree?"

"Wins?"

It was more difficult than she realized. "You want to do 'A' and he wants to do 'B'. Which do you normally end up doing?"

Atulah actually laughed, "Yung, you are being silly. There is usually a 'C' that is better than either 'A' or 'B'. It may just take some time to find it."

Yung pressed, "And one of you doesn't get frustrated waiting to find 'C'?"

She laughed even harder, "And what would that accomplish?"

Most of her questions produced similar results. A class on *Abnormal Psychology* or *Resolving Conflict* wouldn't have any data here, let alone students. She was reluctant to disturb any workers in the fields, so after speaking with a number of others, they were ready for lunch. To complicate matters, there were no children, hence no schools. There was no sickness, so no medical profession or hospitals. Much of what would seem normal on Earth, didn't even exist on Mahdeem. Yet the people were all peaceful, happy, content.

Yung tried, "What do you do with your leisure time, when you are finished working?" Her answer was a blank stare. "What does your husband do when he comes home from working in the fields?"

"I'm not sure I understand what you mean by 'working in the fields?' It is all a cooperative endeavor to produce a crop. You seem to imply a fighting against something. There is no 'fight' here."

Yung tried another tactic, "What do you do for fun?"

This wife, too, chuckled, "It is all fun. We love what we do."

By the time they were walking back to lunch, Yung was thinking, "*It will cause a total transformation of my thinking, but can I stay here?*"

Chapter Thirty-Nine
From the Sky

They were walking through the courtyard when Akilah, Odemel, Cinam, Sheen, Keli, and Labub all ran out of the house.

Odemel shouted, "Quickly, to the compound!" They materialized at their normal spot as Odemel commanded, "Bring them all here, quickly!"

Akilah and Yung ran to the airlock. They emerged to tell Julie, "We need to evacuate. Take only what is necessary." They ran back to everyone's quarters to help. They each collected a bundle of what they thought necessary and Akilah herded them through the airlock.

Then she realized that Dr. Qxilo was not there. She found him at the table in the dining room, having donned his space helmet, and gloves. "Quick, Doctor, we have to evacuate."

He dismissed her with a wave, "I'm not coming, leave me."

She was near panic, "Now!"

Julie appeared next to him. She thought briefly of them just grabbing him.

His words were clipped, "I don't believe you. I'm not sure why I even put on my helmet, here in the middle of the ship. Just go! I will take my chances alone."

Julie shrugged and pointed towards the airlock and mouthed, "*Go!*" to Akilah.

With a final backward glance, Akilah ran to the airlock. It cycled. As she ran out of it, someone grabbed her, and there was a tremendous concussion.

When she awoke, it was dark. She seemed buried. She realized she was beneath Cinam, protected from a pile of rubble. She pinched his arm as she groaned, "Help me out of this."

Then she realized. He wasn't breathing. She wiggled, as she whimpered, "Cinam, Cinam?" Nothing. She scraped the dirt before her face to under her belly.

She broke free into the light and took a deep breath. She called, "Odemel?" and he was suddenly there, digging her out. He finally pulled her free.

She turned back and cried, "Cinam?"

Odemel said softly, "Not now, but he is immortal. He will return"

She looked at him, resignation covering her like a blanket.

She brushed the dirt off of herself, "The others?"

"All made it to safety with the exception of the doctor."

She sighed, "What was it?"

He looked up into the sky, "A meteor. I'm sorry I didn't have time to explain, but the warning was short."

Akilah was puzzled, "But how could that happen here?"

Odemel looked her in the eyes, took a deep breath, and intoned, "All creation groans, waiting for the revelation of the children of God." He continued, "All creation, not just the creation called Earth, awaits the full revelation of all the children of God."

Dr. Qxilo had difficulty recalling exactly what had happened. He was sitting at the table in his space suit. Akilah had left him, running towards the airlock. Suddenly Sheen had tackled him, knocking him from the table. Everything shook, there was a loud noise, a bright light, and he found himself here.

He was standing next to a highway. Looking around, he thought, *"This looks like Earth."* A car was coming up the highway, so he stepped out into the street and put up a hand, meaning, *"Halt!"*

The car stopped, the man rolled down the passenger window, "A little early for Halloween isn't it?"

Dr. Qxilo just shook his head, "Are you familiar with Space Force?"

The man nodded. "Yup, they are just over that hill." And he pointed.

"Could you drop me off there?" Dr. Qxilo said with a very serious tone.

The guy raised his eyebrows, "I can, but it will do you no good. You practically need a letter signed by the President to get into that place."

Dr. Qxilo sighed, "That's fine, just drop me off." The man unlocked the car and Dr. Qxilo struggled into the seat and looked for the seatbelt.

THE END
of the first book
of the
Aries Chronicles

Glossary of Names

Akilah - Aries crew member, a Muslim botanist

Alex- member of the Ying-Yang Development Team

Anavaheem - Martian like berries

Artemis - the first sentient computer, mother of Julie

Ashrah - the amount for Martian purchasing

Ambon - market leader

Atlas - Martian wife

Charash - jewelry smith

Cinam - angelic companion of Akilah

Darah - Martian farmer

Darnah - Martian farmer

Dr, Qxilo - Aries crew member, a Chinese physician

Ginnethon - head of agriculture

Haechad - Odemel's city

Haklayeem - Martian farmers

Inveem - Martian like grapes

Jacob Thomas - Mack's dad, colonel in Space Force

James Irvine - developed an anti-gravity device

Joseph Mendel - accidental creator of Artemis

Julie - Aries Ship's sentient computer (+ Android)

Kadkod - jewel atop Odemel's staff

Keli - angelic companion of Mike

Labub - angelic companion of Mack

Lee Qing - leader of the Chinese Ying-Yang team

Lewis Thompson - head of SSDS

Lianhua - Lee Qing's daughter

Ma-adeem - local name for Martians

Mack - Aries crew member, an American pilot

Mahdeem - local name for Mars

Makael - Odemel's angel lieutenant

Mike - Aries crew member, an American engineer

Molly - Joseph Mendel's assistant

Nefesh - angelic companion of Yung

Norman Packer - Mike's dad at JPL with team of Davis, Susan, Barry, and Karen

Odemel - the angel governing Mars

Nobah - Odemel's serving angel

Rimnon - large Martian fruit

Rukhot - Odemel's serving angel

Sheen - angelic companion of Dr. Qxilo

Taenah - Martian like figs

Tamareem - Martian like dates

Yung - Aries crew member, a Chinese psychiatrist

About the Author

William Siems, "Bill" to his friends, seems to have started telling stories as soon as he could talk. His wife says he still tends to share the truth creatively and with a flair for the dramatic. He grew up in South Seattle and has lived in Tacoma, Washington since 1972.

He worked nine years in hospitals, completing half his RN education. If you had a heart attack, he says he could half save you. Bill joined the Boeing Airplane Company in 1979. The last 15 years of his 32-year career he taught Employee and Leadership Development. Bill often developed and taught his own material. This led to writing numerous short stories and dramas, culminating in his first published novel *Amidst the Stones of Fire* in 2017 and its sequel *Out of the Sanctuary* in 2018.

A Biblical Adventure series followed, named The Chayeem Chronicles. It began with the Christmas adventure *The Magi and a Lady,* and then the gospel adventures *Hane and the Centurion,* and *Zach and a Guy Named Joe*, a rewriting of the first part of the book of Acts.

He then wrote the archangel series, *The Adventures of R'gal the Archangel: The Sword Shenah,* wich was followed by *The Prince and the Soldier,* and finally *Shamah and Anekah.*

He entered contemporary Christian fiction with the series *Before the End: School Daze, Just Joe,* and *Lucy, a Dog, and Her Friends.*

Aries Mission marks his first story in the science fiction genre. There may be a sequel.

Now retired, Bill spends his time teaching, mentoring, writing, acting in community theater, and enjoying his family. Bill and his wife Nancy, of nearly sixty years, live near their children, grandchildren, and finally a great-grand-daughter.

If you can't find Bill in his home office, with pages from his next book strewn all over the floor, then he *used* to be across the street playing with the neighbor's dog, Stacy, to whom he was Dog-father. She, however, has gone on to a better place. (Yes, he believes dogs go to heaven.)

Now he starts his days, six days a week, at a local Chick-fil-A, where he is known as Mr. Bill and is working on book fourteen.